MARVIN & TIGE

by
Frankcina Glass

St.
Martin's
Press

New York

Library of Congress Cataloging in Publication Data

Glass, Frankcina.
Marvin and Tige.

I. Title.
PZ4.G5494Mar   [PS3557.L317]   813'.5'4   77-76634

ISBN 0-312-51783-1.

Tige leaned against the telephone pole in front of the drugstore and reexamined the pad of his left foot through an inch-wide opening in the bottom of his shoe. He looked at his right shoe and saw that the leather was tearing away from the thin black sole to reveal three sockless toes. Knowing he was past due for a new pair, he had in mind the nearly new brown loafers belonging to the white boy he'd been following cautiously for three blocks.

The boy was about Tige's height, a bit stouter and a couple of years younger, which would tend to make getting the shoes from him easier.

Tige watched the boy's mother inside the store waiting third in line to get a prescription filled. He knew he wouldn't have a more perfect time to make his move, so he removed his shoes and placed them in a nearby trash can. Then he pulled off the oversized army jacket that he had borrowed from an army-surplus store and had neglected to return.

He folded the jacket neatly and placed it at the base of the pole, then glanced through the store window to

check on the boy's mother again. She was now browsing
through a magazine as she waited in line.

Tige walked over to the red-haired, freckled-face
boy and greeted him innocently.

"Hey."

"Hi," came the reply courteously, but with the high-
pitched southern drawl that Tige despised yet found so
common among white women and their children. Tige
was fortunate not to have that particular southern charm,
or if he did have it he didn't notice.

"What you doin' out heah?" Tige asked him.

"Waitin' on my mother."

"You wanna play till she comes out?"

"Play what?"

Tige shrugged his shoulders and looked up and down
the empty streets. "I 'on't know. You wanna race?"

"My mother told me not to leave this spot."

"Aw, we can race ten times over befo'e she even
knows what happened. Man, you just chicken, that's all. I
bet you cain't race noway, sissy."

"I'm not no sissy, you take that back!" the white boy
snarled, his red face turning even redder. Tige walked a
semicircle around him and dug his thumbs into the belt
loops of his tight bluejeans.

"Ain't my fault you turnin' into a gull," he said. "Cain't
run, you just cain't run. I bet even if I gave you a head start,
I could still pass ya." Tige turned his back to the boy who
sat deliberating on the tiny ledge of the store. Inside, his
mother was just being waited upon. "Hey, freckles, you
wanna race or not? Beat ya ta that brown car up dare.
Give ya a head start ta the wadder hydrant—"

"I don't need no head start!" said the boy, standing
and ready.

"Okay, okay," said Tige, moving up alongside him.

"But wait—you wearin' shoes, I ain't."

"I can take them off." He slipped out of his shoes easily, removing his socks also. "Okay, I'm ready."

Tige grinned and shook his head. "Man, I still say you cain't run. I'll give you a head start ta that wadder hydrant and I bet a quarder I still pass ya."

"I told you I don't need no head start, but let's see you try it anyway."

"Okay, now when I count three, you start and when you git to the hydrant, I'll come after ya. One... two...three!"

On the count of three, Tige grabbed the shoes, getting the socks as well. The white boy sped away toward the brown car without noticing that his opponent was headed in the opposite direction. When he reached the hydrant, he finally turned his head to see how fast Tige was coming. He came to a sloppy and abrupt halt when he saw his mother with her hands on her hips and a scornful frown on her face. There was no sign of the little black kid who he claimed had stolen his shoes.

Three blocks away, Tige stopped to try on his new shoes. They were a size too large, which was good. He'd have a better chance of wearing them out first before he outgrew them.

With one main task completed, Tige thought of another he had to see to. He slipped the army jacket on again and proceeded down the street to the A&P on the corner. He hadn't been there in quite a while, so he didn't expect any problems. He had been careful not to go *anywhere* too often. He didn't want to become recognized as "that kid again"—the one that picks up things, sticks them in his pockets, and disappears without paying. Fortunately, he had always been careful of what, how, and where he did his stealing.

He had worked out a system for using the reinforced
lining of his jacket as a shopping cart. He'd walk around
the store quite freely and examine cans and packages as if
trying to decide whether or not his mother would buy
them for him. Then when he was sure of himself, he'd
place the item on a shelf about knee high and while
pretending to examine another article with his right hand,
he would slide his left hand through the hole in the pocket,
take the desired object, and store it in the lining.

Once he had collected all he could without getting
noticeably plump, he would head for the store's parking
lot, where he'd offer to help other people with their
groceries. When he was allowed to load the groceries into
the backs of cars, he would carefully slip articles out of the
bags—preferably meats, since they were harder to get
inside the store. Some people would think him so sweet
for helping, they'd tip him a quarter or more, which he
would pocket happily. Only after his jacket was full
would he return home.

Tige's home was on the second floor of a two-story
apartment building consisting of six one- and two-
bedroom apartments. To get to it, he sneaked onto two
buses through the back doors and then strolled down
sidewalks cluttered with hopscotch marks, dirty words,
and broken liquor bottles.

Some people might hesitate before walking down
these streets past the winos and the too obvious ladies of
the evening with their long blonde or brunette wigs, their
willowy legs, and their faces caked with makeup.

Tige would just snoot his nose at them and they
would snoot back, cursing him for being such a smart-ass
kid. He'd return their curses and scare them by throwing
rocks—intentionally missing. But knowing his mama
would be expecting him, he didn't torment the ladies too

long, even though they expected it each time he walked
by. When he walked by quietly and greeted them with a
smile, they reacted the same way, knowing that it was
only another one of his ways of aggravating them.

Tige strolled closer to home, a rock flew past him
about three feet off target.

"Tige!" a loud voice shouted from behind him. "Tige,
you bedder gimme my quarder back, man!" Derek tried
to make it sound like a threat, but Tige ignored him. If
there was one person he didn't have to worry about, it was
Derek. Derek was only seven-and-a-half years old—a
mere baby to Tige—and his only threat was to run tell his
mama, who never seemed to care anyway because Derek
was forever telling something on somebody.

"I want my quarder back, man!" he yelled at Tige.

"Told you a hundred times, sissy, I ain't got yo'
quarder," Tige said calmly.

"I ain't no sissy, and you *is* got my money too, 'cause I
laid it on that step and turned 'round and you picked it
up."

Tige stopped a moment and turned to face him.

"Listen, you see me pick up that quarder?"

"Nawl, I had my head turned."

"Then how you know I got it?"

"'Cause you was the only one dare."

"But you still didn't see me git it, did ya?"

"Nawl, but . . ."

"Shut up then—you cain't prove nothin'." Tige made
his point and continued walking.

"I'm still gonna tell on you," Derek pouted.

"Tell, smell, go ta heaven," Tige replied.

"You old stankin' nigga!" Derek shouted. "Yo'
stankin' mama wear army boots!"

"That's all right," Tige said as he started up the steps

of his apartment building. "Yo' stankin' daddy wear Kotex."

Derek's eyes widened and he threw his hand up to his mouth.

"I'm gonna tel-l-l-l-l," he threatened, then ran back down the streets. Tige snickered lightly, thinking to himself that he'd like to be there when Derek offered his parents that bit of information. He turned and continued up the green-colored concrete steps to the porch and stopped to investigate his mailbox.

He knew they only received two kinds of mail—junk, and bills. He preferred the junk mail. Though he was never able to afford the goodies it offered, it didn't cost him anything to look. He went through the two doors of the building into the hall, and as he started up the stairs, he ran into Mojoe coming down.

Mojoe was four years older than Tige and a big pain—nosy, big-mouthed, and a pain. He was wearing dark shades and had a cap drawn down over the left side of his thick Afro. A freshly lit cigarette dangled from his fat dark lips.

"Hey, Tige, my man. What's *hap'nin'*?"

"You ain't, that's fo' sho'."

"Aw, my man, why you wanna be like that? I'm just tryin' ta be friendly."

"Okay then, gimme five dollars, *friend.*"

"I would if I could, you know."

"Yeah," nodded Tige, "but you cain't, 'cause you ain't. I done heard that befo'e."

Mojoe placed his arm around Tige's shoulder as they climbed the stairs together.

"Man, you know if I had it ta spare, I'd give it ta ya."

Tige stopped to glare at the hand that rested on his right shoulder, then turned his gaze on Mojoe, whose body was only inches from his.

"You must don't wanna keep yo' arm attached ta the rest of yo' body, do ya?" he asked. Mojoe removed his hand and arm promptly.

"Cain't nobody even touch ya, can they?"

"You wanna touch somebody, go play with yo'self," Tige said. He started off alone, only to have Mojoe follow.

"Hey, I ain't gotta play with myself—I can git a chick anytime I wanna. All I gotta do is... whistle."

"Yeah, whistle and all them dogs come runnin'."

"Speakin' of dogs—yo' mama got a dude with her: fat, *ugly* son-of-a-bitch too."

"Mojoe, why 'on't you mind yo' own business sometime?"

"Just tryin' ta keep in the news, that's all. By the way, my man—how much do yo' mama charge? I thank I might wanna buy a piece myself." Mojoe grinned, displaying a gold filling and a broken tooth.

"Go ta hell, Mojoe."

"Hey, squirt, you 'on't be tellin' me where ta go. I'll go up side yo' head with my fist, Jack."

Tige finally became fed up with Mojoe's presence. He spun around suddenly with a short-handled switchblade clicking open in his hand. Mojoe jumped back startled, as Tige eyed him coldly.

"What was that you just said?" Tige questioned.

"Nothin'," Mojoe grinned nervously. "I ain't said nothin'."

"Well, what was that about my mama?" Tige asked him, keeping a tight hold on the handle with the point of the blade beneath Mojoe's chin.

"I was just jivin' 'bout that. You know me, I was just jivin'."

"That's what you want me ta tell 'em ta put on yo' headstone? Heah lies Mojoe. He ain't really dead, he just jivin'."

"Cool it, li'l' bit, just take it easy. You want me ta 'pologize? Okay, I 'pologize. I was just jokin'. You know me."

Tige knew Mojoe all right. He was always joking and jiving, running off at the mouth and sticking his nose into other people's business. Mojoe stepped cautiously away with a stupid grin tacked to his face. "Catch ya later, li'l' bit." He waved his hand and ran down the stairs. Tige put his knife away and started down the hall. Believing what Mojoe had told him about there being a man with his mother, he passed by his own apartment. Although he hated Mojoe, he had no reason to disbelieve him.

He strolled casually along the hallway, noticing that the couple two doors up were at it again. The only thing worse than having drunks for neighbors was having *married* drunks for neighbors. Mr. and Mrs. Willis Hicks were chronic alcoholics who had been married for twenty-three years. They fought every other night in the week.

The discussion this night seemed to revolve around a bottle of bourbon that Mrs. Hicks had drunk without permission. She said that since Mr. Hicks had left it in his drawer for so long, she figured he didn't want it. But *he* claimed that he had just put it in there two nights before.

Tige leaned against the wall opposite their door listening to them quarrel. They threatened to leave each other, or to kill each other, but he knew they'd never do either one. Tige found them entertaining at times. He recalled the day Mrs. Hicks had tried to force her husband to leave; she didn't like the way he looked at other women. She asked what they had that she didn't, pointing out that while she wasn't a spring chicken, she still had what she started out with twenty-three years ago, if not more. She held the door open for him, forgetting that she herself was stark naked.

When she finally heard all the snickering and whistles from her neighbors, including Tige, she slammed the door and proceeded to accuse Mr. Hicks of putting her on display. That was true love for you.

"Ev'nin', Tige."

"Ev'nin', Miss Carrie." Carrie Carter stood with the key to her door in her hand. She shook her head as she looked toward the Hicks's door.

"Them folks oughtta be 'shamed of themselves carr'in' on like that. Is yo' mama home, Tige?"

"Yeah, but she busy though." Carrie nodded understandingly.

"Well, you tell her I said hey."

"Yes, ma'am."

Tige watched silently as she unlocked her door and went inside. She was a nice lady, he felt; a nice dresser too when she had time to sit at her sewing machine. Not very pretty though, but as far as Tige was concerned, forty-year-old women who'd gone through as much as she, had the right not to look like beauty queens. He liked her just the way she was. He couldn't stand her son Mojoe, but he had nothing against her other three kids. He was often invited over to watch television since he didn't have one at home, and when he was younger, Carrie used to baby-sit him. Now, at age eleven, he didn't consider himself a baby any longer. He was perfectly capable of taking care of himself when left on his own, but it was nice to know that if he should need it, he'd have someone to turn to for help.

He looked down to his apartment when he heard the door open. A black, forty-some-odd-year-old man with a fat stomach and balding head stepped out. Tige recognized him as the man to whom he had talked the day before. He looked like the businessman type, even though he didn't exactly dress the part. Still, the simple slacks and shirt he wore had to cost about thirty dollars; watch, about

a hundred; shoes, at least forty-five, and wedding ring—
who knows?

He smoothed down his hair—a wasted act—then
checked his watch. He probably had to be home before
the little woman got suspicious, Tige thought, turning
away in disgust. He hated the idea of this fat, ugly, bald
old man being with his mother, and he wished desperately
that she wouldn't keep selling herself like that. But
Vanessa had sat him down and explained everything to
him. She went slowly and told him of how she must
manage to keep a roof over their heads. It was a very hard
task she'd had to do alone nearly since he was born, and it
had become more difficult when she was laid off her job a
year ago.

She had been working in a poultry house, slaughter-
ing and packaging chickens. It was a messy and back-
breaking job that had taken quite a lot out of her. Her
hands had had numerous cuts and calluses where she had
been using heavy scissors to cut the chickens. Constant
bending over the vats had given her back trouble. The
plant was always damp and cold, which had added to her
discomfort. But despite everything, she knew that she had
a son to support, so she had kept with it for as long as she
could.

It had been one of the few jobs she had ever held. She
had worked there for ten years—there seemed to be
nothing else she knew how to do. When the plant had
closed down, she had been left jobless. It was just as well,
Tige thought. He had never liked how she used to work
herself so hard. It showed in her face. She was only
twenty-nine, but she looked older—even her hair was
prematurely graying. She complained of aches and pains
all over her body, and she looked pale, sometimes almost
lifeless. He feared that she was very sick. He had asked her

to see a doctor but she had refused. Years before she had suffered from an ulcer and she also had high blood pressure. Tige never really understood what either of those were. He knew only that they were bad for her. At first, she took pills constantly; finally she had had an operation.

She swore to God that that was her biggest mistake ever; her operation had marked the beginning of their financial problems. Blue Cross had taken partial care of the hospital bills, but there was nothing to cover her other debts. The payments on the refrigerator, the stove, and the furniture for the living room and Tige's room added up to a few thousand dollars and rent and utility bills added to the load. She blamed herself for running up so many bills. She had tried to get too much too soon and had ended up over her head in debt.

Now she decided that she'd rather live with the pain and discomforts of her recurrent illnesses than take the time needed to make herself better. She thought that if she stopped working long enough to regain her health, she would end up losing the few possessions she had left. Tige disagreed with her, but remembering the sting of painful face slappings, he was afraid to tell her she was wrong.

He gave her a few more moments to straighten up or whatever she did after a customer left. When he entered, she was changing the sheets on the bed. "I'm home," he announced without receiving a reply. He walked to the kitchen table and began to empty his jacket. Vanessa finished with the bed and came to examine what he had brought.

"I hope you brought somethin' that don't need cookin'. They cut off the gas taday."

"We can still use the hot plate, cain't we?" Tige asked.

"Oh, I didn't even thank of that. Go plug it in fo' me.

I'll fry some spam and open up a can of po'k and beans—is that okay?"

"Yeah, that's okay."

Tige turned on the hot plate while she put away the groceries and started dinner. Thirty minutes later they sat down to eat.

"I see you got some new shoes. Where'd you git 'em?"

"This stupid li'l' white boy I got ta race with me barefooted."

"They look like they oughtta last fo' a while."

Tige lifted his pantleg. "I got the socks too," he said. "I sho wish I could've seen it when his mama come out though."

"Well if she can affo'd ta buy..." She took another look at the shoes and calculated a figure. "If she can spend 'bout fifteen dollars on a pair of shoes, she can prob'bly buy another pair just as easy. You come across any mo'e customers fo' me taday?"

Tige shook his head with his mouth full, then cleared it enough to speak.

"Nawl. It was some who wanted ta, only they couldn't spare the money. One guy asked if you'd take credit cards. He was just full of bull, that's all. How much you make taday?"

Vanessa grunted and shook her head. "I only had three. That's fo'ty-five dollars. Still ain't got anough fo' the rent. Damn, this dump."

"Maybe you oughtta charge mo'e," Tige suggested. "Them women down on the co'ner charge 'bout twenty-five or thirty dollars."

"Well, I ain't nothin' like one of them wenches down on the co'ner. I'm a beggar and beggars cain't be choicy. I do well ta git what I *am* git'in'. I know I ain't no fashion model and everybody else know it too. My hair turnin' gray, my feet swell up, my back aches—ain't even thirty yet and I'm already set fo' the grave."

"I can go sell some papers tamorrow fo' the rent money," said Tige, trying to divert her thoughts.

"Well, if you don't git much, don't worry 'bout it. If this rathole don't burn down befo'e Wednesday, we'll just wait and pay the late charge on it."

His mother, he noticed, had a certain way of looking at things. She preferred to live life one day at a time. She didn't like jumping too far ahead into a future that might not be there.

"What all you been doin' taday—besides what I see you been doin'? You have a nice day?"

"Yeah, all right I guess. I went out ta Greebriar. They got all they Christmas stuff up now."

"Christmas," Vanessa sneered. "Just another excuse ta drive folks in debt. Oh well. I'll see if I cain't git you somethin' this time. I cain't promise you though."

Tige nodded understandingly. His past Christmases hadn't been very bright as far as toys were concerned. He agreed with his mother that it wasn't worth spending that kind of money on things that wouldn't last a month, though he secretly dreamed of owning a bicycle or a pair of skates. Until someday when they could afford it, he planned to keep his feelings to himself.

"How would you like one of them little cars that you whip the co'd out and sparks come out of it?"

Tige shrugged his shoulders and smiled shyly. "That'll be okay. I thank they cost about five dollars though—I'm not sure."

"Yeah? Well we got ta save up some because you need a coat too."

"I already got a coat," Tige spoke with a mouthful of pork and beans.

"That thang ain't heavy anough ta keep a moth warm. You need a heavy winner coat. Need ta git you some clothes too so you can go back ta school. Ain't no need fo' both of us ta stay ignorant. Gonna have ta git out and go ta the Salvation Army sto'e and see what they got ta fit you."

Tige frowned. "I 'on't like none of them clothes they have. Most of 'em shirts and pants older than I am and if you do find somethin' that look like anythang, it's always too big. They 'on't never have nothin' ta fit me right." He looked up and saw Vanessa staring at him crossly with an expression that told him better than words to shut up. He did.

"Now you listen ta me: the only reason you got clothes in the first place is ta cover up yo' skinny, li'l' butt-naked body. If you had been bo'n ta be a fashion king, you'd be it already. Child, I do the best I can fo' ya—I just cain't do no mo'e."

Tige hated it when they got into discussions about himself. It always ended with the same results. She'd feel bad for not being able to take better care of him, and he'd feel bad for making her feel bad.

"What you want me ta git you fo' Christmas?" he asked in an attempt to get her mind off troubling thoughts. She smiled timidly.

"Baby, what I want fo' Christmas, they ain't got a box big anough. But anythang you wanna git me is all right as long as nobody catches ya with it. Last thang in the world I wanna have ta do is come git yo' ass outta jail."

She took a sip from her glass of water and crossed her eyes at the sound of an echoed clap accompanied by the squeak of a rat in pain. "Damn! That's the third one taday. Thank they oughtta have sense anough now ta stay away."

"I thank what it is," hypothesized Tige, "is when one leave they hole and don't come back, they send out

another ta go look fo' him. It'd be good if we had a Pied
Piper take 'em and dump 'em in the river."

"Well, till he shows up, you g'on and dump that one.
Wait a while till he's good and dead first."

Tige nodded okay while licking his plate clean of
pork and bean juice.

"You want any mo'e?" Vanessa asked.

"Nawl, I'll save it fo' tamorrow."

"I'll finish readin' that story fo' ya if you wash the
dishes fo' me."

"Okay."

"And I want you ta take a bath tanight. I know you
ain't had one all last week."

"I ain't got dirty yet."

"Dirt ain't got ta *git* on ya, it can *grow* on ya. You can
have the tub after I git through."

Vanessa went off to bathe as Tige did his chores. He
finished up hastily, especially with the removal of the
deceased occupant of the rattrap. It was the fattest rat
he'd seen so far—as long as his forearm. Tige rolled him
up in newspaper and pitched him out the window, nearly
missing the dumpster below. Then he waited his turn in
the tub and afterward, pulled on a brand new T-shirt and
briefs, which, like his shoes, had been long overdue for a
change.

He picked up his Cinderella coloring book—the one
his mama had promised to finish reading—and glanced
through it to find the place they'd left off. It was a thick
book, messily half-colored, that he had found in the park.
It had about three or four lines of type on each page that
explained the story, but Tige's reading ability was limited
to memorizing numbers, bus, and store signs and a few
labels on packages. His failure to complete anything other
than kindergarten and first grade had taken its toll. He

took his book back to the living room and climbed onto the bed next to Vanessa, who was all set to turn in after the story.

"Now where did we leave off?" she asked.

"Right heah. We was comin' up close ta the end."

"Well, this picture heah is where the prince decides ta go all over the countryside ta look fo' Cinderella and he's gonna try this shoe on all the gulls around ta see if it fits any of 'em. Now, he goes ta Cinderella's house. See, he tries the shoe on her stepsisters right heah."

Tige examined the pictures carefully. "Them horses oughtta know they cain't git they big foots in that shoe."

"Now heah's where Cinderella tries on the slipper and it fits. And heah, her fairy-godmother returns and casts the spell on her ta make her all dressed up ag'in. The prince has found his bride and together they ride off to the palace where they are soon wed and live happily ever after. That's the end."

"But what happened to the stepsisters and her stepmama?"

"They 'on't say. What do you thank happened to 'em?"

"They all threw up?"

Virginia broke out in a grin. "You crazy, boy. G'on in dare and go ta bed."

"It's too early ta go ta bed."

"Don't give me no backtalk, just do what I told ya."

If there's one thing that Tige had learned over the years, it was always to obey his mother because it wasn't against her nature to knock him silly if she found just cause to do it. He took his book and started off.

"Ain't you fa'git'in' somethin'?" she called after him.

Tige frowned grumpily as he slumped back to her.

"You wipe that frown off yo' face and come heah.

You only got one mama as if you didn't know. I didn't halfway 'preciate my mama when she was alive neither."

"I 'preciate you," Tige tried defending himself. "You just kiss sloppy, that's all."

He could see that what he'd just said made no difference to her, so he surrendered unconditionally and allowed her lips to touch his. She always preferred kissing on the lips; short, simple, and regrettably wet since she always felt the need to moisten her lips first.

Tige disliked the slobberiness of kissing, and if given the opportunity he would just as soon have wiped his mouth and spit afterward. There were times, however, like now, when he just had to live with it.

Unexpectedly, this time instead of just letting him off with a goodnight kiss, she grabbed and held him close to her bosom, kissing his forehead and patting his back. When he finally emerged for air he looked at her curiously.

"Cain't I even be motherly if I wanna?" she asked, then took hold of him again. "You all yo' mama's got, Tige."

She sounded a bit teary, but when he looked up again she showed no signs of crying.

"Go on ta bed, boy."

He started for his room, then turned to stare at her. He felt that something was wrong and he wanted to ask her, only she spoke first.

"What? You want another kiss?" she grinned. With that, everything seemed fine. He snickered, shook his head, and left.

Tige rose early Tuesday morning, conscious of the rent money he had to raise. He dressed, threw a little water on his face, then went into the kitchen to eat a piece of leftover Spam for breakfast. He moved about quietly so as not to wake his mama—she seemed to need so much sleep lately.

Tige finished his Spam, washed it down with a glass of water and slipped into his jacket. "I'm goin'," he announced by reflex, regardless of whether she was asleep or standing there watching him leave.

He hit the streets to start his paper route. He had a sensible—if not unique—system for cutting out the middleman. He'd get to the paper boxes early, insert his own money, and instead of taking only one paper—as was expected—he'd take them all and sell them while on his way to the next box. Some people even depended on him for their morning papers. He tried hard not to disappoint them and he tried extra hard to be careful—careful not to be caught and careful not to overdo it. Of course, the newspaper people expected to lose a few papers with those idiot machines of theirs, but if they found that they were losing too many, then they might be forced to secure safer measures against theft. That, for Tige, would be a terrible loss of income.

Tige floated across town the whole morning and finally quit after grossing a sum of thirteen dollars and fifty cents. He didn't know that that was how much he had; his arithmetic was at the same level as his reading. But he knew it didn't matter how much he had just made, because they would still need more to go with it.

Before he went on to other things, he stopped for lunch at a hamburger stand. He ordered two large hamburgers and an order of french fries and waved a thumb to indicate that the unsuspecting person behind him was going to pay. He stuffed one of the burgers into the lining of his jacket to save for his mama, then traveled to the park to enjoy his meal.

It was a slightly cool but sunny day. Tige indulged in an hour or two of solo playing on the playground, then used the remainder of the day trying to line up customers for his mama. It was getting harder nowadays to drum up business—maybe because it was getting colder and the days were shorter, or maybe because it was getting closer to Christmas. Men were staying home out of the cold and dark and perhaps saving their money for the presents and bills that came with the holiday season.

After an unsuccessful afternoon of flashing a nude picture and asking gentlemen if they were interested, Tige returned home tired and disheartened that he wasn't able to score anything for his mother.

He entered and announced he was home without noticing at first that Vanessa was still asleep on the bed. He thought it was a bit peculiar for her to be sleeping this time of day, but he didn't bother to disturb her.

He detected a stale, decaying odor and assumed that another rat had been caught in one of the traps. He went into the kitchen and checked them. All were still intact— no little bodies about. Tige opened a window to let in some fresh air, then continued to sniff out the origin of the sickening odor. He followed it into the living room to his mother's bed and squatted down to look beneath it, expecting to find something moldy or dead. There was neither.

He lifted his head and noticed that the odor was much stronger above the bed.

"Mama?"

He climbed partially onto the bed and placed a hand on her arm. Even through the blanket that covered her, he could feel the cold hardness of her limb. He tried to turn her over on her back, but she was too heavy and too *stiff*. Then he flung the covers back from her face and gasped.

His stomach heaved, and he felt the need to vomit. He slid backward, falling onto the floor, then picked himself up quickly and ran out of the room. He went across the hall and pounded heavily on Carrie's door. Mojoe answered it and stood grimacing down at him.

"Hey, runt, what's the big idear?"

Tige opened his mouth in an effort to speak but nothing came forth. Tears flooded his eyes and streamed down his cheeks as he pointed a trembling hand toward the open apartment.

Carrie came to the door and looked at him and knew instantly that something was seriously wrong. She crossed the hall and went inside. She was heard to say repeatedly, "Oh, Jesus," then came out closing the door behind her. She took Tige's arm, moved him into her living room, and sat him down on the sofa while she made a phone call.

His mind raced back to the scene that had just taken

place. His mother, stone dead, stiff as a board with her eyes frozen open. The sight of her lifeless face and that deathly stench returned to haunt him, and the need to let it all come up became pressingly uncontrollable.

He threw his hand up to his mouth and dashed for the bathroom. The perspiration dripped heavily from his pores as he remained perched on the edge of the bathtub for twenty minutes.

There was a commotion outside in the hall when two uniformed policemen followed by two white-jacketed men carrying a stretcher arrived. Tige went to the door and watched as they conferred with each other, jotted down notes, nodded their heads, and agreed that it had been a natural death.

Carrie went to talk to them, explaining that there was no other next of kin except for Tige and that she would take care of him for the night. The officers nodded and stepped aside for the white-jacketed men, stretcher, and body to pass.

Tige stared at the corpse, covered from head to toe with a white sheet. He was oblivious to stares and whispers from his neighbors and of Mojoe's arm around his shoulders trying to comfort him. His gaze followed the men with the stretcher as they began to turn the corner to go down the stairs. He wanted to follow them, but someone was holding him back, trying to turn him away. He moved toward the open door of his apartment and broke free of Mojoe's grasp. He ran inside and locked the door behind him.

The tears broke out once more, but he didn't attempt to wipe them away because he knew they'd only be replaced by more. He looked around the darkening half-empty room. The living-room sofa and tables had been repossessed a month ago, and the place looked so deserted. He looked over at the bed and came to the conclusion that his mother must have died sometime during the night. He could see that she hadn't been out of the bed all day. Her slippers were in the same position on the floor as she'd left them last night, and her housecoat lay stretched across the foot of the bed with one sleeve hanging over the edge just as he remembered.

He went to sit on the edge of the bed despite the scent of death surrounding it, then he heard Carrie's voice as she knocked on the door.

"Tige. Tige, come on out of dare, baby. You shouldn't stay in dare, it ain't good fo' ya."

She paused a moment to listen for a response.

"Tige... I know how you feel, but... well, why 'on't you just sit fo' a while, honey. You can come out later and spend the night with me, all right?"

She waited for a reply but none came. She decided to give up for now and leave him in peace.

As his tears began to dry, Tige wondered to himself what he would do now. The state would probably take him and place him in a home of some kind. He didn't think he'd care much for an institutional home—to have his freedom obstructed and his ways changed.

He thought for a minute of Carrie, but she wouldn't want another kid. She had enough trouble with the brats she already had. If he were put in an orphanage, he knew his chances for adoption were slight. Actually, it didn't really matter what happened to him now. There wasn't much of a reason to go on any longer. There was nothing left for him here; he would have to leave.

He went into his room and gathered up as many of his personal belongings as he could push into his jacket. Then he gave the apartment a once-over, silently saying farewell to it. He went through his mama's closet and examined her shabby dresses and shoes. There was not much to remember her by—no special little token he could keep with him, no photo album filled with pictures of her face.

He dragged himself to the door, knowing that there was nothing to keep him now—no reason ever to come back. Living in this unfurnished rathole had left him no fond memories, unless someone would consider carrying out dead rats, stomping finger-sized cockroaches, and standing by to watch your furniture being taken away as fond memories.

The only reason he had bothered to stick it out was because of Vanessa. He would have done anything for her, she had only to tell him so. He never knew before how much he had loved her. He never told her so, but perhaps by some chance, she knew it anyway.

He opened the door a crack to make sure the coast was clear. He had no intention of spending the night across the hall. It wouldn't do him any good; they would only hold him until the proper authorities came and took him away. The halls were empty, so he took the opportunity to leave quietly.

Dusk was beginning to fall outside, and it was turning cooler. Tige stepped slowly, almost daydreamingly along the streets, trying hard not to bump into anything and having little success. He didn't even bat an eye when a car screeched to a halt to keep from hitting him and the man inside cursed him loudly for not watching the lights.

Tige stopped and looked back blankly at the intersection. So what if the car *had* hit him? What if his insides had been splattered all over the pavement? Who would really give a damn, he wondered. Perhaps the person who hit him would feel something. He would probably feel anguish for taking another's life, never knowing that he had just done that person a favor. That wouldn't be right though—to hand over the job to someone else. His life was his own problem, and he'd have to take care of it himself.

He turned away from the cars and walked—since he was headed that way—into the park. He walked along an area of the lake that was deserted, except for the ducks and swans that floated beautifully way out in the center. Tige watched them with sadness. They, combined with the blue-black sky and the tops of trees reflected off the water, made a beautiful scene. It was one of his mother's favorite things to look at. She rarely came to the park, but when she did, she loved to watch the lake until darkness made the reflections impossible. She got so few pleasures from life that small things like this easily made her smile.

Tige moved closer to the edge of the bank and looked over. He felt a minor urge to dive into the dark, murky water—to slip below the surface and not return. A few short moments would put an end to the miserably lonely life he had before him. The thought of dying became impressed in his mind. What he was thinking made him feel scared and confused. He needed to sit down and think things out. He looked out across the water again and then to the other side of the lake, observing that now he had company. He could see the distinct figure of a man pulling a small wagon. The man stopped to dig into a trash can, pulled something from it, and threw it into his wagon. He would probably grow up to be like that, Tige thought—a grown man salvaging other people's trash.

He turned from the lake and walked along a footstone trail until he came to a bench where he sat to ponder his dilemma. He tried to count the reasons why he should stay alive. He could take care of himself well enough if it came to survival, but he would never have a decent place to call his home.

He thought a little about orphanages. He wasn't sure he could get along with other children. It had been so long since he'd been around them or had had time to stop and play. No, he wouldn't like an orphanage, where he'd either be caged until he was eighteen or palmed off on strangers; he doubted that anyone would want to adopt him anyway—at least he knew *he* wouldn't.

The reasons for dying seemed to outweigh the reasons for living. If he just called it quits now, he thought, at least he wouldn't have to worry tomorrow about the things he was worrying about now.

He reached down into his pocket and pulled out his switchblade. He sprung it open, stared loosely into it's shiney reflection, then inched up the sleeve on his left arm to expose his wrist. He held the edge of the blade steadily against the biggest of the veins, inhaled and exhaled deeply, and wondered what the hell he was waiting for. He thought perhaps an angelic voice would speak out from somewhere and tell him that his life was much too precious to throw away. He expected a fairy-godmother, a beautiful woman in a flowing white gown covered with stars, to appear before him and ask him of his troubles. It would be so much simpler if things happened that way, but for some stupid reason they just didn't. There was no use in delaying it any longer. He took another deep breath in preparation for the pain he expected to feel any second.

"I bet that's going to smart some," came the nonangelic voice of a man somewhere in the mid-darkness. It wasn't enough to startle Tige for he didn't even hear it at first, but it *was* enough to distract him.

"In fact, I'm pretty sure that's going to hurt. You know, if you're going to go, that's really one of the most painful ways."

Tige let the blade slip a few inches away from his wrist and looked over to the man who had just taken a seat beside him. It was the same man whom he'd seen pulling the wagon on the other side of the lake.

"The thing wrong with that," he continued, "is that you bleed to death, and some people are slow bleeders. You could lay around three or four hours before anything happens, and that's a long time to be suffering. Then there's the chance that somebody could get you to a hospital in time, and the doctors could save your life. That in itself would be a big waste of effort on your part. Then after they plugged your leak, the next step would be to call on an expert for advice—by that I mean a psychiatrist. Now, he's going to want to probe and search and see if he can't find out why a little eight- or nine-year-old kid would want to kill himself."

"'Leven," Tige stated softly out of automatic hatred of being incorrectly referred to.

"Excuse me. Eleven. Eleven, they would think—just a year from twelve and puberty, when you start getting hair on your chest and muscles, and grow to be six-feet tall. They would wonder why an eleven-year old would want to give up all that. But being psychiatrists, they would think they already know. They would say he's undoubtedly unhappy about something. Maybe there's been some tragedy in his life that he can't cope with. Maybe something or *someone* in his life, *isn't* anymore."

Tige dropped his head and raised it a second later.

"My mama dead." He offered the information nearly in tears.

"Oh. I'm sorry to hear that," said the stranger apologetically. "I really am. Was she all the family you had?"

Tige nodded once.

"I can see how that can make a person feel lost. I can see easily. I saw you when I was over there. You looked as though you were going to jump into the water. That's a lot simpler than what you have planned here. What happened, did you change your mind?"

Tige shrugged his shoulders and shook his head, indicating that he wasn't sure.

"Now see, you're off to a bad start there. You weren't sure of yourself then—you're probably still not sure now. You should never make big decisions that way. You have to be one-hundred percent sure one way or the other. Don't just say, well maybe—I guess so—why not? Because you only have that one time; you don't get a second chance. For instance, if you want to die, I can suggest some other ways—then you can pick and choose. You won't have to do a spur-of-the-moment thing. Let's see—there's gas, electrical shock, jumping from a building, sleeping pills, poison, hanging, and if you knew where to find a gun, there's the reliable old bullet through the head which rarely, if ever, fails.

"But on the other hand, if you want to stay alive, at least for the night, I could invite you over to my place and feed you a bowl of chili. You could get yourself some rest—sleep on it—and start over in the morning. That's the way you should do things."

Tige sat motionless with the blade completely away from his wrist. He had just about given up the idea of doing himself in after hearing all the trouble he'd have to go through if he didn't do it right; not to mention, listening to the gory ways that he had to choose from. The more he thought of it, the worse it seemed.

"Has anything I've said made a dent?"

Tige gazed up at the face of the man beside him. He was a blue-eyed, brown-haired, stubbly-faced white man with liquor on his breath. But the warmest of expressions appeared on his face when he smiled.

"Would you like to come home with me?" he asked. "You don't have to if you don't want to, but you really shouldn't stay out here all by yourself. The boogieman might get you."

"Ain't no boogaman," Tige told him.

"Well, you may be right. I wouldn't know. I never stay out long enough to find out."

The man stood up—he was over six-feet tall—and reached for the handle of his wagon.

"Coming?"

Tige sat for a while watching him walk away. Then he folded up his knife and followed a few steps behind him. He looked back along the trail that had become dark and a bit spooky. He didn't believe in monsters or boogiemen, but there was something about the dark that he never appreciated. He quickened his pace and kept within a short distance of his new acquaintance.

After a long walk in an unfamiliar neighborhood, the man picked up his wagon filled with empty soft-drink bottles and newspapers and began to ascend a flight of stairs toward a small apartment over a boarded-up store. Tige waited cautiously at the foot of the stairs while the man opened his door and switched on a light. He looked down at Tige and smiled.

"Thank you for standing guard. There's not too much violence in this neighborhood, but you can't always be too careful. I think it's safe enough to come up now."

Tige moved up the stairs slowly. He stopped a foot from the door and peered in. The room was furnished tackily with a sofa bed—already let out—end tables, lamps, and a coffee table sitting upright in a corner. A dinette set filled the tiny kitchen, which someone had neglected to partition off from the living room.

"It's not much, but it keeps the wind out. Come on in."

Tige stepped inside the door and felt an immediate
surge of warmth, welcome relief from the cool night air.
"Sit down, make yourself at home. By the way, I'm
Marvin Stewart. A terrible name, Marvin, I know.
Whenever I think of someone with the name Marvin, I
always picture a guy with thick black glasses, a plaid suit,
a little bow tie, and brown shoes with white socks."

Marvin stopped talking long enough to pull off his
coat and hang it in the closet. He put his wagon away in a
corner with a stack of ten full crates of bottles.

"I'll turn those in tomorrow. You can make pretty
good money off bottles. That's about twenty dollars'
worth right there. Only problem is that they're making so
many no-refund, no-return bottles, the regular ones are
hard to find. But whenever someone's giving a party or
something, I manage to pick up quite a few. Why don't
you have a seat while I warm up a pot of chili I made fresh
yesterday."

Tige looked about casually as Marvin began to
scrounge through his refrigerator. Then he took a seat at
the kitchen table, which seemed to be as good a place as
any, and watched the man called Marvin as he went about
warming up his meal.

He seemed a nice enough man. He could only be one
of two things, Tige thought. Either he was a kind person
who opened his heart and door to a fellow human in need,
or he was a perverted sex maniac who devoured young
boys, taking first their bodies and then their lives.
Somehow it didn't matter which he was. At the moment,
he was being the first of the two, setting an aluminum-foil-
covered skillet on top of the stove and saying something
about it that Tige didn't pay attention to.

He was a constant talker without a southern accent—
a mature man with streaks of gray in his short and shaggy
hair. If one looked at him long enough, one might go as far

as to say he was handsome, or that he *could* be if he fixed himself up.

"Oh, I'm sorry if I talk too much for you. That's generally what happens when you place a tenth of the dictionary's words in front of some people. Would you like to take your coat off? The only really good thing about this place is that it's easy to warm up in. No drafts."

Tige shook his head no, slid back in his chair, and folded his arms across his chest.

Marvin turned his attention to the chili that was slowly simmering. "Ahh, just about ready. You *will* join me, won't you?"

Tige stared at him without answering.

Marvin looked away and went to the sink, where he reached for two plates from a pile of dirty dishes, squeezed some dishwashing liquid on both, and rubbed them clean under running water. He took them to the table, where Tige sat with his head bent low, sniffling.

"Hey...don't do that, don't cry. But...on second thought, I guess it does help if you let it all out. Because you know what makes you cry?—not just you, anybody. It's your thoughts, your feelings, that do it."

Tige raised his head and glared at him again.

"Now you see, all your thoughts are right up here." Marvin touched his forehead. "And when you're thinking sad thoughts, bad times, misery and all, it triggers a special reaction. All your good feelings go through a separate channel and that's why you laugh and smile, but when these depressing, aggravating, sad thoughts collect, it's just like decongesting a head cold. You know when your nose begins to run? It's doing a little of it now. Well, those thoughts begin to drip, run straight down your forehead out your eyes in the form of tears. So the more you cry, the more of those feelings you get rid of, and the sooner you start feeling better.

"See?" He pointed to Tige, indicating that he had stopped crying. "Some of those bad feelings are gone already."

He picked up the potholder and wiped away the wetness from Tige's face.

"There. Feels a little better now, doesn't it?"

Tige fixed his gaze on the man, totally taken in by his words. No one had ever given him an explanation for crying, and this one seemed as true as any he would ever hear because what Marvin had said seemed exactly like what was happening. Now that some of the tears were out—added to the fact that he was in a nice warm place— it did make him feel slightly better.

"Yo' stuff's burnin'," he said.

"What?"

Tige pointed a finger to the stove.

"Oh no!" Marvin leaped to the stove in one bound and grabbed the pot from the fire. He looked at it once, frowned, and threw the whole thing into the sink. He put his hands to his waist and shrugged his shoulders.

"Well, so much for dinner. I'm afraid I didn't do my grocery shopping this week," he said apologetically as he took his seat with a pout. He looked on as Tige dug down into his jacket and brought forth a large hamburger wrapped in white paper. He placed it in front of Marvin and sat back quietly.

"For me? What about you?"

"I ain't hungry."

"Well, thank you very much. You sure you don't want half?"

Tige shook his head no.

Marvin pulled the paper from the burger and ate it slowly. "By the way..." he asked between swallows, "whom have I had the pleasure of dragging home with me? What's your name?"

"Tige."

"Beg your pardon?"

"Tige."

"Oh, Tige. Is that a first or last name?"

"First. My last name Jackson."

"Tige's a handsome name. It's unusual though. Is it African?"

Tige cocked his head to one side and scowled. "You see a bone stuck in my nose?" he asked.

"I didn't ask if *you* were African, I only...never mind. Where's your father, is he dead too?"

"Might be, I 'on't know. He ain't never been around that I know of."

"He and your mother divorced—do you know?"

"Ain't never been married I 'on't thank. I asked mama one time where my daddy was. Everybody else had one 'cept me. She said I ain't never had none. Then I found out later on how people git chillun and I asked her ag'in where my daddy was. I knew I had ta have one some time or other. Then she said I got a daddy all right but that he 'on't give a damn 'bout me 'cause as far as he concerned, we dead."

Tige yawned, not bothering to cover his mouth, and closed his eyes sleepily.

"If you want to lie down, the bed's right there."

Tige looked at the dirty-sheeted unmade bed and threw an 'are you kidding' glance at Marvin, who immediately got to his feet and swooped all the covers off.

"Sorry about that. You can see I don't get much company."

Marvin dumped the dirty linen into a corner of the kitchen, and from the closet he pulled out fresh ones. He spread two sheets and a blanket across the bed and tucked the corners in sloppily.

"How's that?—better?"

Tige pulled off his jacket without answering.

"You got a bathroom?" he asked.

"Certainly. Right through there."

Tige laid his jacket on the back of the chair and went off to the bathroom. When he returned, he saw Marvin recapping a liquor bottle and sticking it into a drawer. He took a half glass of whatever was in the bottle back to the table with him and sipped it slowly. It occurred to Tige then as he slipped out of his clothes that the fellow was on the verge of being drunk, though he hid it very well. A happy drunk; that would account for his gracious attitude and his talkativeness, and for his constant smiling.

"You mind music?" Marvin asked, standing by a radio on one of the end tables. When Tige shrugged his shoulders, he switched on the radio to an instrumental version of "Moon River."

Tige climbed into bed and adjusted his pillow. He looked at Marvin, who was watching him silently. Small dimples showed on each side of Marvin's face, and his blue eyes let out a tiny sparkle somehow. It was kind of cute, Tige thought.

"Would you like the light off?"

Tige shook his head no and rolled over on his side. Marvin smiled to himself. "Goodnight to you too."

Tige awoke to the snoring of the man asleep beside him. He got up and dressed quietly, used the bathroom, and left without a word.

The day was sunny, a crisp forty-five degrees. A few little leaves were still clinging to nearly bare trees.

"It's winnertime, you dummies," Tige muttered. "*Fall,* stupid. Dumb leaves ain't got *no* sense."

Tige looked about to get his bearings. Marvin

obviously had few neighbors. The rear end of a trucking company was across the street, taking up the whole block, and only an empty house and an air-conditioning company occupied Marvin's side of the street. No doubt he didn't have to worry about privacy.

Tige trudged down the stairs, zipping up his jacket securely. He picked a direction to take, not caring where it would lead him. His only incentive was to keep moving. He didn't feel half as bad as he had the night before, but then again he still didn't feel that great either. He needed to keep his eyes roving and his mind moving. He didn't want to give himself a chance to stop and think back. He walked at a fast pace, then finally broke into a trot. He wouldn't stop until he had to.

Tige spent a good part of the morning doing what he did best—roaming. He hopped on a couple of buses and allowed them to take him wherever they were headed. He let his eyes stare out the window, seeing things but not bothering to look at them. He was still scared and confused, and he still had no idea of what he would do with himself. He broke out crying again, and an aged white lady sitting beside him asked what his problem was. He rang the bell to let him off at the next stop, wiped his eyes, and told the lady to mind her own damn business.

When he got off the bus, he found himself downtown. After his cry, like the man said, he was feeling a little better. And listening to a comical conversation between three girls while awaiting the light to change added to his lifted spirits. He couldn't bring himself to smile but at least it helped to chase away his solemnness.

He crossed the street and upon reaching the other side, he passed a blind man—a highly familiar blind man who wasn't quite so blind the last time he had seen him. The man was wearing dark glasses and had a white cane in one hand and a tin cup in the other. Tige looked him over curiously.

"Now what's all this 'pose ta be?" Tige asked him.

"Beg your pardon?" said Marvin, not bothering to look at him.

"I said what's all this about? You wa'n't blind last night."

"Well, all this bright sunlight is *very* blinding."

"You standin' in the shade though. Man, you ain't nothin' but a jive con man."

"Oh, no. You're quite wrong there. The way I understand it, a con man is a fast talker, a fast thinker, and a man who tricks people out of their money. Me, I'm neither a fast talker nor thinker, and I don't trick people out of their money. I merely stand here with my dark glasses, my cane, and my cup. I don't beg; I don't ask for a single solitary dime. But if people passing by feel it in their hearts to give a little of themselves, I could certainly use the dough."

Tige accepted that as an honorable statement. "How much you make doin' that?" he asked.

"Well, actually I don't do it very often. I'm mostly a handyman when I can find the work. But when things are a little slow and the bills are due—on good days, I can make about twenty dollars, sometimes a lot less. Say, I wonder if you wouldn't do me a favor."

Tige looked at him suspiciously. "What?"

"Something very simple. I want you to play a game with me. See if you can't ease a couple of fingers into the cup without touching the sides, and pick up a quarter. Go ahead—bet you can't do it."

Annoyed that Marvin doubted his skill, Tige started to comply, whereupon a huge, hairy, pale hand clamped suddenly about his wrist.

"Put that back, you little thief." The husky, stern voice of a stout, white businessman startled him into dropping the coin. He looked to Marvin for help, but Marvin was playing the role of a blind man totally bewildered by the small commotion.

"This kid just tried to steal your money," the man said to Marvin.

"Really? I had no idea anyone was even there. So quiet."

"Yeah, he's sneaky all right. You wanna apologize to this man, sonny?"

Tige thought about what he really wanted to say but decided to hold his tongue. Instead, he simply threw his left shoe into the man's shin and escaped his clutches.

The man cursed under his breath and rubbed his leg a bit.

"If I could catch him now, I'd really show the seat of his pants something. That's what's wrong with them these days. Their folks too afraid to show them who's boss."

"Well," said Marvin, "maybe he really needed the money."

"There's better ways of getting it than stealing from the blind," grumbled the man as he took out his wallet, pulled a five-dollar bill from it, and placed it in Marvin's hand. "Here's five dollars. You put that in your pocket and be careful from now on. People do anything for money these days."

"Thank you, sir. Thank you very kindly."

The gentleman walked away and Marvin looked slowly around for a sign of Tige, who returned a moment later, very much annoyed. Having run completely around the block, nonstop, he was breathing heavily and spoke with short, quick breaths.

"Man . . . I could . . . kick yo' ass fo' that!"

"Do that, and I'd probably change my mind about taking you to lunch. Thanks to you I'm five dollars richer. Would you care to walk me down to Blimpey's? Just take my arm and pretend you're guiding me. Makes you look humane."

"Humane? I ain't no dog!"

Marvin smiled amusedly. "I believe you have it a little turned around. You're thinking of the Humane Society, which deals with animals. Humane itself doesn't mean dog *or* animal; it means kindness—kindness to animals and to your fellow human beings. But it doesn't matter. I don't think anyone's paying any attention anyway."

Marvin slipped off his shades and put them into his pocket along with the little cup.

"Come along. I'll buy you a Coke and a double-decker sandwich of your choice."

Tige walked behind him peacefully, then moved up closer.

"Hey, I thought you said you wa'n't no con man. What was that you just pulled?"

"That? I have no idea. First time I've ever done anything like that. Just came to me all of a sudden. I'm glad you were smart enough to run, and I do apologize for using you that way."

"Just 'on't try it ag'in."

"Don't worry.... So, what have you been doing today?"

"Nothin'. Roamin'."

"Roaming makes you feel better?"

"Yeah. I was just ridin' 'round on the bus."

"Did you find a place to stay yet?"

"I ain't looked. But if I wanted to, I could just git myself locked up in a sto'e or somewhere. I did that befo'e."

"You plan on doing that forever? Really, it wouldn't hurt any if you turned yourself over to the welfare people, or whoever handles things like that. Let the state take care of you."

Tige frowned. "I wouldn't go ta them people fo' nothin'."

"Why do you say that?"

"Welfare thank they somethin'. They always want ya ta come beggin' to 'em. You gotta do what they say or they won't help ya."

"Well, how about straight to an orphanage? Maybe some nice family will adopt you."

"Who gonna adopt me?"

"Someone perhaps. Why? Are you that terrible to get along with?"

"Nawl, I ain't terrible. But when people adopt, they wanna li'l' baby, somebody they can raise up the way they wanna. I'm too old ta be changed."

"No one's ever too old to be changed. Look at me—I've changed considerably."

"Yeah, I can see that. I didn't thank you was a drunk bum *all* yo' life. You talk too good fo' that."

"Hey, where're you going? This is Blimpey's."

Marvin opened the door and allowed Tige to enter first. They each took a stool at the counter and waited for a chance to order.

"I think I'll have me a tuna fish sandwich on white and a cup of coffee," Marvin ordered when the waitress came to them. "What would you like, Tige?"

"I wanna ham and cheese, a bag of potato chips, and a large orange drank."

Marvin smiled. "I see your appetite's back."

"I ain't had nothin' ta eat taday. But like you was sayin' about changin'—wa'n't you somethin' bedder than what you is now? How come you changed ta worse?"

"I'm afraid that's rather a long story to tell."

Tige propped his elbows on the counter and fixed a steady eye on Marvin. "I ain't in no hurry. I got loads of time," he said.

"Hey, you ain't from Atlan'a, is you?"

"No, I'm from a little ways up north—Detroit."

"I heah that's a cool place. Why'd you leave?"

"Too many memories in Detroit. That's where I was born, where I went to school, where I met my wife and raised my family..."

"Yo' family dead or somethin'?"

"Just my wife. About eight years now. Then there's my children...." The waitress came with their food at that moment.

"How many you got?" Tige asked casually, then attacked his ham and cheese as soon as the waitress let go of the plate.

"Three, if I remember correctly. Two boys and a girl, whom I don't hear very much from."

"What's the madder? They 'on't like you or somethin'—or 'on't *you* like *them*?"

"Very perceptive lad. That, I wonder myself. I don't know. They took away my wife from me. She'd always say there'd be plenty of time for us after the children were older and could look after themselves. They didn't love *me*, only what I could buy them or do for them. When their mother died...things changed. She had been the key to what held us all together, and once she was gone, so was everything else. We started drifting apart until finally we went our separate ways. My daughter's married, Keith's a doctor, and David wants to be a rock star."

"Why you pick Atlan'a ta come to?"

"Oh, I was sent here by my company to work at it's Georgia branch. It's an advertising firm. I was pretty hot stuff back then. They liked me because I was so good selling over the phone. It was a hassle though—really. I just got frustrated with the whole nine-to-five bag. Getting up at six to fight the traffic to make it to work on time, filling out reports, business luncheons, trying to impress some fat cat loaded with money, and the boss always wanting more than he's paying for. 'Let Stewart handle this—let Stewart take care of that.' I really got fed up with the whole thing. At least before, I had a reason to go through all that. I had a family to support, but then there was just me. And one day when my alarm clock didn't go off and I was two hours late for work, I said to myself, so what. I never needed that much money to live off anyway. All I needed was a roof over my head and enough for food. So I sold my car and my golf clubs and I got out of that rat race. I don't even miss it any. I'm satisfied living simple and just being my own man."

"Sounds pretty stupid ta me," said Tige as he completed his meal. "But I guess I would've had ta have somethin' ta know what it's like not ta want it. I'm ready ta go."

Marvin finished his coffee and paid the bill. He followed Tige out slowly.

"Where are you headed now?" he asked.

"I 'on't know. Just around, I guess. Where you goin'?"

"Well I have a few odd jobs to do today. I have some painting I have to do for a lady. Probably take about four or five hours. I could get through sooner if I had a little help. I'll pay you thirty percent of what I make."

Tige stuck his hands in his pockets and shook his head.

"I 'on't feel much like workin'. I thank I'll just do some mo'e walkin'," he said as he began drifting down the street.

"Tige," Marvin called to him.

"Yeah?"

"If you need a place to stay tonight, I hate to think of you just out here with no place to go."

"I can take care of myself."

"I'm sure you can. Well, see you around then."

Marvin went his own way and Tige went his. He swiped a candy bar and moon pie from a newsstand arcade and went to Rich's department store to spend the rest of the day. He picked out his favorite color television set and sat down Indian-style on the floor to watch a murder mystery. But he became a little too carried away with his viewing and soon found the man who turns off sets, turning off the sets. It was ten minutes till six, ten minutes before closing. Tige had planned to get himself locked up in the store. But it was out of the question now; he had waited too long to lose himself. He would be told that the store was closing, then he would be watched by a man on each floor as he came down the escalators, and finally a last man would watch him go out the only door open.

He stood there in the cold dimming dusk. At least there were still people about. Traffic was still moving, buses coming and going, people going home after work.

Tige leaned against a silver-colored lamp pole with his hands deep inside his pockets and watched the people, all of them waiting for a bus or a ride to take them home. Home. It finally occurred to him that he wasn't going home, that he no longer had a home to go to. He'd always considered himself a big boy, someone who could easily take care of himself. But right now, he felt like a very little boy, lost and alone.

Now that he thought of it, he was frightened. He had nowhere to go. He thought for a second of Carrie. But he couldn't go back there, across the hall from a dead woman.

The people around him started to disappear little by little and the traffic steadily decreased. He pulled himself away from the pole and began walking. He could think of only one place to go. If that idea failed, he was left with just one other solid solution to his problem.

He arrived at his destination in an hour and stood gazing up at the lighted windows for a full five minutes. Then he climbed the stairs with soft steps and tapped on the door with tiny cold knuckles. He tapped louder when his first announcement went unheeded.

"Who is it?"

"Tige."

"Who?"

Tige puffed annoyedly. "How much *comp'ny* do you *git*?"

Marvin opened the door and stood holding onto the knob.

"Well, hello again," he said, noticeably surprised.

"Hey," said Tige shyly. He looked through the door past Marvin, then down at his own feet.

"Oh! Where are my manners? Come on in. It's cold out there, I know."

Tige slipped in and moved over to the heater.

"You look like a cold soul," said Marvin. He sat down on the bed where he had apparently been lying and reading a book. "I take it you didn't find a place to stay tonight—other than here."

Tige looked away, embarrassed.

"That's all right. You can have another night. I remember I invited you. It gets quiet around here sometimes. I could use the company. Are you going to try again tomorrow?"

Tige shrugged his shoulders haplessly. Marvin nodded and scratched the side of his nose.

"Well-l-l . . . I guess . . . why don't you pull your coat off. I won't bite. You'll get warm enough."

Tige shed his jacket reluctantly.

"Closet's right there."

He hung it on the doorknob.

"Mm uh. That way you can see if anyone steals it, or for *a fast getaway?* I noticed you weren't as cautious last night. But then again you weren't really feeling yourself, I suppose. It's good to be cautious, though. There're a lot of dangerous people in the world these days. You have to be careful of them. I'm not saying I'm not one of them, because I'm not so sure that *you're* not one. But I do give people the benefit of the doubt. I do allow myself to trust sometimes. I trusted you not to bash my head in last night in my sleep and ransack my humble abode. Some of the things around here could bring good money."

"I 'on't steal," Tige blurted. "Not from people who ain't hardly got nothin'."

"That's comforting to know, but it's not quite what I was getting at. I was merely trying to get you to see something: if I have no reason to be afraid of you, then you have no reason to be afraid of me. *Are* you afraid of me?"

Tige bit his bottom lip and kept his eyes on the floor.

"That's interesting. I assume then that you are and you aren't. You are because you barely know me, and you aren't because you need a place to stay. Commendable. Anyway, you're welcome to stay here for awhile—that is, if you want to. That's up to you until you get your head straight about what you want to do with yourself. Are you interested?"

Tige glanced up and nodded his head slightly. Marvin stretched out on the bed and picked up his book. "There're a couple of fish sticks left in the pan if you're hungry," he said, then resumed reading his paperback novel.

Tige fed his hunger with a fish stick sandwich and a glass of water, then sat at the table with his hands folded in front of him. Bored, he looked about and yawned silently. Marvin looked up from his book.

"Sleepy?"

"Nope."

He drummed his fingers on the table unconsciously.

"I can see you're not having the greatest of times there," said Marvin, not being able to concentrate on his literature.

"You ain't got no television, is you?"

"Not unless it's invisible. I have a radio. Not as exciting, I suppose. I have a deck of cards. Would you like to play?"

Tige shrugged his shoulders. "Okay."

Marvin went to the chest of drawers and picked up a deck of worn cards.

"You know how to play poker?" he asked as he returned to Tige.

"Nawl, I 'on't know that."

Marvin handed the deck to him and took a seat opposite.

"Well, what would you like to play?"

"You know how ta play old maid?" Tige asked as he began to shuffle the cards quite clumsily. Marvin looked at him in surprise.

"What's the madder with you?"

"Nothing. You just surprised me, that's all. I sorta thought . . . I mean, I figured that you knew all that stuff—you know, cards, dice, gambling, everything."

Tige thought a moment and tried putting himself in Marvin's place.

"Oh."

"Oh, what?"

"You must thank I'm like Mojoe."

"And who's Mojoe?"

"Stupid ol' creep who live 'cross the hall from me. You know where Boulevard is? You know, down dare near Ebenezer Church?"

"You mean with the Martin Luther King Memorial? I have a good idea where it is, but I've never had much reason to go down that way. Is that where you live?"

"Yeah, 932 Boulevard. Anyway, what you talkin' 'bout is Mojoe. He fifteen years old. He do all them thangs: play cards, roll dice, smoke, drank, take dope, mess with gulls—he do everythang. You know how ta play old maid or not?"

"It's been a long time but I think I can manage it. Deal the cards."

Tige shuffled through the cards, removed the queen of clubs and tossed it aside. "This," he said, holding up the queen of spades, "is the old maid."

"Okay, I can remember that."

Tige began to deal and continued the conversation as if he'd never interrupted himself.

"Mojoe gonna end up just like his brothers. He got a brother nineteen and one seventeen. The one nineteen in the peniten'try fo' shootin' and killin' a man in a crap game and the one seventeen in reform school fo' stealin' a car. Miss Carrie got her hands full with them niggas."

"Miss Carrie's their mother?"

"Yeah. 'Pose ta say Mrs. Carter, but I never do. She got a good job; she work where they make ink pens, and she was savin' her money up so she could buy a house and move outta that neighbo'hood. She was gonna let me and my mama come live with her—you know ya 'pose ta pull?"

"Pull?"

"The cards. You take out all yo' pairs first, then we take turns pullin' from each other."

"Okay, I've got you."

"But Miss Carrie had ta use the money she saved ta git her dummies a lawyer. She didn't trust the ones the cou't try ta give ya. So, she never got her house. When mama died, I thought 'bout askin' her if I could live with her."

"You like her a lot?"

"Yeah, she's okay—you pull first, then I'll pull. She used ta baby-sit with me when I was li'l'."

"Last year, huh?" Marvin joked.

"I mean when I was a kid, you know, 'bout fo' and five years old. I hated it, though, when her and mama got ta talkin'. A earthquake couldn't shut 'em up. What makes gulls talk so much anyway?"

"You're asking me? So why didn't you try going to Miss Carrie for help instead of running amuck trying to do yourself in?"

"I was feelin' bad then, you know. But I figured she wouldn't want me no way 'cause of all the trouble she already got. Plus ta adopt somebody, you gotta have a good house and a husband. Her husband dead."

"I'm sorry to hear that," said Marvin, then he grimaced as he pulled the old maid from Tige's hand. Tige smiled slyly and continued.

"I thank I would've like livin' with her if it wa'n't fo'

Mojoe. That nigga ain't gonna never 'mount ta nothin'."

"What about you? What do you think you'll amount to?" Marvin asked while trying casually and unsuccessfully to return the old maid to Tige.

"Me? I ain't worried. I might not make it ta twelve, much less try and 'mount ta nothin'."

"That's a pretty rough thing to say."

"So. It's true though. Look what happened ta my mama. She knew it wa'n't no good ta try and plan nothin' fo' the future 'cause she knew it wa'n't comin'. Didn't see her savin' up fo' no retirement. She never got a chance ta retire."

"But that *is* where she went wrong; not planning for the future—at least for yours, if not her own. She didn't leave you anything, did she? No home, no money, and no one to look after you."

"Prob'bly 'cause she knew I was gonna follow her. I almost did, ya know. I still might. Man, I just won the game."

"You did?" Marvin noticed the lone queen in his hands. "Oh, I'm the old maid. Well, let's try it again. This time I'll deal. And by the way, if I were you, I wouldn't dwell on the subject of death so much. See, there might be a reason why I came along just when I did. Maybe I'm your guardian angel sent to watch over you."

Tige looked at him solemnly, then shrugged his shoulders.

"I ain't gonna knock it, maybe you is."

"*Are,* not is," Marvin corrected him.

"Are, not is, what?"

"You are, not you is. You don't use *is* with you."

"How come? It mean the same thang, don't it?"

"Yes, but that's not the way it was intended to be."

"Well, I could care less. Least I ain't talkin' like no

baby. Ain't nobody ever had trouble understandin' what I'm talkin' 'bout. I 'on't see what the hell you complainin' 'bout either."

"Is it necessary for you to have to curse?"

"Grown-ups cuss."

"Not all of them. And I, for one, don't as a rule. I just wasn't raised that way. It sounds vulgar enough coming from adults, but it's worse coming from children."

"Well, where you thank chillun git it from in the first place?"

"I won't argue about it. I just don't want to hear any more of that kind of language coming from you."

"You 'on't be tellin' me what ta do," Tige said crossly. "I say what I wanna."

"You say what you want to but not in front of me. If you plan to stay around here, let's get one thing straight right now. This is my home and what I say, goes. If you don't like the idea, there's the door."

Tige cocked his head to one side and spoke back challengingly.

"I ain't gotta do nothin' you tell me and I *ain't* gotta stay heah."

"That's true on both accounts—or is it? Just ask yourself why you stepped through that door in the first place. The last resort, isn't it?"

Tige splattered the cards on the table and went for his coat.

"I'm leavin'. I ain't gotta take this."

"Where will you go?" Marvin asked in the same tone of voice he used when Tige arrived.

"Who the hell cares?" Tige snapped, hastily zipping up his coat.

"I suppose I do . . . a little. Don't ask me why, because Lord knows I haven't the faintest idea. But it's too dark and too cold for you to be wandering around out there. I know you don't have any place else to turn, otherwise you would've done so. Stay. We can try and meet each other halfway on things; not all your way, not all mine, okay?"

Tige stood by the door and stared at Marvin unyieldingly.

"Well, see, that solves one problem right there. As long as you're not talking to me, you can't swear me out. I'm going back to my reading. You do what you like."

Tige stood there lamely, showing marked symptoms of indecisiveness and fear. Marvin pretended to ignore him, and kept to his book, but watched his movements from the corner of one eye. Tige placed a hand on the doorknob and twisted it slowly. He deliberated quite some time before letting go. He pulled off his jacket and laid it on the back of a chair, then looked back at Marvin, who turned another page in his book.

"I'll leave in the mo'nin'."

"If that's what you want," Marvin nodded.

Tige sat at the table and gathered up the deck of cards. He devised a game to play by himself and played quietly until he heard Marvin's gentle snoring. Then Tige got up and joined him.

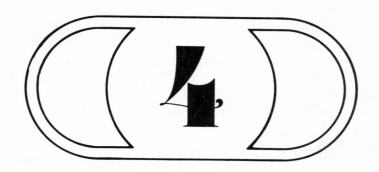

"Well, good morning," Marvin greeted Tige as he crawled out of bed and into his clothes. "I thought maybe you might like a little breakfast before you left."

Marvin placed two bowls on the table and filled them from a cereal box. "Wait a minute and I'll get the milk."

Tige took a seat at the table in front of one of the bowls and stared blankly into it.

"Now just what's this 'pose ta be?"

"That's shredded wheat. Haven't you ever had any before?"

Tige frowned. "It look like straw."

"Just because it looks like straw, doesn't mean it tastes like straw." Marvin drowned the cereal in milk and added sugar for him. "Try that," he said. "See how you like it."

Tige picked up his spoon and tried to find a sensible way to spoon up just a little of the straw. He used his fingers to try and break off a piece of one of the biscuits.

"You can't eat it if you're going to play with it."

"I ain't playin'!" Tige snapped and let the biscuit drop back into the milk. He folded his arms away from the bowl and glared at Marvin. "You ain't got nothin' bedder'n that?"

"Well I never claimed to be Aunt Jemima. Most of the time I don't even eat breakfast. But this stuff is good for you, it's nourishing, and it's all I've got. If you want something better, you'll just have to go out and get it yourself."

"Where's a sto'e open?"

"Ah . . . two blocks down and turn to your left. They don't give handouts in case you're interested."

Tige ignored his last remark. He got his jacket and emptied it of his clothing, placing all the articles in a neat pile on the bed. Marvin watched silently, impressed by how much Tige could fit into it.

"Don't mess with none of my stuff," Tige warned as he slipped into his jacket and headed for the door.

"I take it then, you *will* be back?"

Tige only gave him a wayward glance as he closed the door on his way out.

Twenty minutes passed before the door reopened and Tige stepped in empty handed.

"I could have told you that you'd need money when you walk into a store these days. Good thing I didn't eat yours too."

Tige ignored Marvin's smirking grin as he went to the table and unloaded his jacket. Marvin watched with amazement as a small box of instant grits appeared in Tige's hand. Next came a package of sausage, a half-carton of eggs, a stick of butter, and a roll of biscuits. He looked at Marvin and smiled lightly.

"How's that, Aint Jemima?"

"That's . . . that's what I call breakfast."

Tige pulled off his jacket, and Marvin watched him curiously.

"Can you pull a rabbit out of there?"

Tige smirked and shook his head.

"Did you by any chance pay for that, or do you have a charge card?"

"What do ya thank?"

"That's what I thought. You know it's not really a nice habit to steal."

"Might not be nice but it's bedder'n starvin'."

"But hasn't it ever occurred to you that you might get caught?"

"All the time. That's why I'm careful. If it bothers ya, you ain't gotta eat none of it. You can finish yo' li'l' wet straw dare."

Marvin studied Tige's intended bowl of shredded wheat and nodded. "I'll try not to let it bother me too much. Let's fix some breakfast."

Tige assisted graciously with breakfast by setting the table and doing the dishes.

"We make a pretty good team," Marvin stated as they sat down to the fullest meal either had had in quite a while.

"What grade are you in school, Tige?" Marvin asked casually.

"Why?"

"No particular reason. But I *was* wondering what you were going to do about returning to school. Since you don't have a legal guardian, that's going to be a bit of a problem, isn't it? You do want to go back to school, don't you?"

"Not partic'ly. I couldn't go if I wanted ta anyway."

"Why is that?"

"'Cause I got kicked out."

"Why were you kicked out?"

"'Cause I played hooky too much."

"Any particular reason for that?"

"Hey, man, let me eat this stuff fo' it turns molded."

"Sorry, go ahead."

Marvin ate silently along with Tige, whose appetite seemed twice his size.

"I had ta quit school ta help my mama pay the bills," Tige said finally.

"Oh, you had a job?"

"I had lots of jobs. I had ta go out and get the food all the time."

"You mean like you did this morning?"

"Yeah. Sometimes we paid fo' it. But we never had much money. Mama didn't have no job. They laid her off where she used ta work and she tried ta find a job but she never could."

"So you decided to quit school and get a job," Marvin hypothesized.

Tige looked at him, annoyed.

"You thank you know the story, why 'on't you finish it?"

Marvin apologized and asked Tige to continue.

"Well, my mama was kinda weak, you know. Her foots swelled up all the time and her back hurt her and she was ti'ed a lot. It wa'n't much she could do, so I started doin' what I could without git'in' in trouble. But I never made much, so Mama, one day she asked me ta do somethin' fo' her."

Marvin felt that Tige was about to shy away from his confession, so he asked, "Was it something bad she asked you to do?"

Tige stared down into his empty plate and answered quickly and softly, "I pimped fo' her."

Marvin raised an eyebrow, wondering if Tige actually meant what it sounded like he said.

"You were your mother's *pimp?* You mean hustling on the streets?"

Tige nodded shamefully. Marvin didn't know what
to say.

"You didn't like doing it, did you?"

"Nawl. But if I didn't, she wouldn've just got out dare
and did it herself. She said that was all that was left. If that
was the only way ta keep us from starvin', she'd just have
ta do it."

"Well, what about welfare? Didn't she have some
form of social security she could draw on?"

"Welfare wa'n't anough. We had all these bills. I 'on't
know 'bout nothin' else."

"Well . . . uh, isn't there a lot of money in prostitu-
tion?"

Tige sighed and shook his head sadly.

"Not if you ain't got a good pimp and not if you 'on't
look all that good. Mama was kinda plain. She wa'n't like
them others who strut around on the co'ner with they skirts
up over they hips and they tops all fallin' out they blouses.
They all look like trash, but I guess that's what guys like
best. With mama, I had ta go out and tell some dude 'bout
her—make her really sound good—and once they got to
the 'partment it'd be too late fo' 'em ta turn back. Besides,
she charged less. They figured they was git'in' a real
bargain anyway."

Tige fell silent, staring grimly down into his lap.
Marvin watched him sympathetically, trying to think of
something appropriate to say.

"You miss her, don't you?"

"Yeah, I miss her. She was still a good mama, I 'on't
care what nobody say. She cooked fo' me whenever she
could and whenever I was sick, she stayed up all night and
took care of me."

He paused a moment to think.

"Marvin?"

"Yes?"

"They make ya go ta hell fo' bein' a prostitute?"

"They do consider it a sin. But I think they'd also consider all her good points too. She'll probably make out all right. . . . Ah, well . . . can't just sit around here all day. I have to go pay a bill."

Marvin left the table and went to the chest of drawers where he pulled out his wallet and began examining its contents.

"I should have paid it yesterday," he said, "because it's due today. And old Georgia Power is closed today, but maybe if I slip it into the box, they won't cut off my lights."

He took the wallet back to the table along with the bill.

"Let's see now. At least I *think* I have enough. Twenty-eight, thirty-two. That's not bad for two months."

He counted out the money quietly and came up four dollars and thirty-two cents short.

"Mmm. How did that happen? Oh yeah, the five from yesterday—forgot I spent it. Oh well. Say, you wouldn't happen to have four dollars and thirty-two cents on you, would you?"

"You promise ta pay me back?"

Marvin looked up in surprise. "You mean you have it?"

Tige rummaged through the pocket of his jacket and brought forth a tightly tied plastic bag. He struggled to get it open, emptied out a handful of quarters, and spread them out on the table.

"How much ya said ya needed?"

"Four-thirty-two."

Tige tried for a moment to calculate that, then gave up.

"Git what ya need," he said.

Marvin wiped up all but ten of the quarters.

"I'll pay you back soon as I can, I promise. But tell me. If you had money all along, why didn't you use it to buy food instead of stealing it?"

"If I hadda got caught stealin', *then* I would've used the money ta pay fo' it. Make sense?"

"Makes a lot of sense I suppose. Well, I'm going to dump these dishes in the sink and run downtown. You want to come along? Or..."

Tige shrugged his shoulders.

"I ain't got nothin' else ta do. Might as well."

Marvin deposited his payment in the light company's mail slot and walked along the streets lazily with Tige trailing him.

"How come it's so quiet all over?" Tige asked him. "Where *is* everybody taday?"

"It's a holiday, didn't you know? Today's Thanksgiving Day."

"Thanksgivin'? Already?"

"I see you've lost track of time. I suppose everyone's over at Grandma's house or Aunt Jane's having a family reunion. What kind of Thanksgiving do you generally have?"

"Miss Carrie cooks a lot of stuff and she invites me and my mama ta eat with her."

"Is she a good cook, Miss Carrie?"

"Man, you bedder know it! She have food comin' and goin': turkey, dressin', potato salad, candy yams, collard greens, co'n on the cob, cranberry sauce...man, them plates be packed, jack."

Marvin smiled at the enthusiasm with which Tige delivered his description of a more than adequate meal.

"Think maybe she saved a place at the table for you?"

"What?"

"I was just thinking that maybe you'd have a nicer day if you spent Thanksgiving with her."

Tige stared off to his right with a scornful indentation over his brow.

"Did I say something wrong?" Marvin asked.

"I ain' *never* goin' back dare," Tige said, and he looked defiantly at Marvin. "And you ain't gonna make me either."

"No, I wouldn't make you go. I just thought that maybe since she's such a good friend of yours and she lives right across the hall from you and your . . . Oh. I see now. I put my foot in it, didn't I?" said Marvin softly after finally realizing Tige's reluctance to return to his origin. "I'm sorry I brought it up. We just won't talk about it anymore, okay?"

Marvin walked along quietly, then stretched his arms and clapped his hands together.

"Since it *is* a holiday, you have any idea of what we could do?"

"I 'on't care," Tige mumbled, disinterested. "I wanna see the parade," he said suddenly.

"What parade?"

"The one they have on Thanksgivin'."

"Oh, you mean Macy's. You want to go to New York and see it or just on television?"

Tige eyed him with annoyance to let him know that his question didn't deserve an answer.

"That's what I thought. Let's go find a television set."

Tige followed Marvin as he'd always done since they'd met, cautiously and always a few steps behind, still uncertain as to whether he should put his complete trust in him.

"Here we go," said Marvin as he held open the heavy door of a dimly lit bar.

"I can go in dare?" Tige asked him.

"Sure. Nobody'll mind. I think. Go on."

They entered the establishment and took stools at the bar. Tige gaped about the room trying to adjust his eyes to the dimness. There were only five others besides the bartender—two men having a friendly card game, a hooker making her move to pick up a fellow, and a gentleman in the Geritol segment of life drooling over a martini.

The bartender, a stout, Jewish-looking man, gave Tige a passing stare as he greeted Marvin.

"How ya doin', Marv?" he said with no trace of a Jewish accent.

"Hi, Ed. Figured you wouldn't let something like a holiday stop you from making money."

"The wife's left me anyway, so . . . Say," he pointed to Tige. "He wouldn't happen to be a twenty-one-year-old midget now, would he?"

"Oh, Tige. No, he just wanted to watch the parade on your set, if you don't mind any."

"Mind? Why not. I would've already had it on but I was busy at the time."

Ed turned and reached over a shelf of glasses to switch on the sixteen-inch set hidden by the sliding panels of the wall.

"Thanks, and how about a little scotch and water for me?" Marvin asked. "Put it on my bill?"

"You're running up a pretty big bill, you know?"

"I always take care of it, don't I?"

"Yeah, I guess so. Anything for the little one? Ginger ale?"

"With ice," Tige stated emphatically.

"On the rocks, coming up."

The bartender prepared their orders and pulled a bag of potato chips from its stand to give to Tige.

"On the house," he smiled, then stood by to watch the parade with them.

"I wonder what would happen if one of those big balloons exploded? If somebody stuck a pin in it or something."

"I don't know. Seems like it'd blow everyone away," Marvin speculated. "It'd probably be like a short-winded tornado. But I suppose they make them out of pretty strong material because I've never heard of it happening."

"Tell ya one thing—I'd sure hate to be the one who has to blow 'em up."

"I don't blame you."

"And another thing—you know them rose parades? Ain't no way in the world they could git me to pluck ten-thousand rose pedals for no float."

"That *is* a lot of work," Marvin agreed. "But those people really do some beautiful work."

Tige gazed at the colorful screen, trying all the while the two men were talking to dub out their voices and tune in to what the announcers were saying. He finally looked at the bartender who was trying to ask him a question.

"What's Santa Claus gonna bring you for Christmas?" he was asking.

"What San'a Claus?" Tige answered. "Ain't no San'a Claus."

"Well, who do you think is riding in this parade?"

"That's just a fat white man with a fake beard and a pillow tied ta his stomach. Ain't no real San'a Claus. That's just what y'all got yo' chillun believin' so they'll be good fa a coupla weeks. Y'all got money, y'all can do that, but people ain't got no money, it just make 'em feel bad 'cause they cain't git nothin'. Ain't no such thang as a San'a Claus, so dammit, y'all need ta stop tellin' them lies."

"Tige," Marvin scowled disapprovingly. "That's no way to talk to people. I think you owe Ed an apology."

"Hah," Ed waved his hand. "Kid's right, he's right."

"Well, right or wrong, he should have a bit more manners." Marvin spoke to the bartender but kept his eyes on Tige.

"Don't bother about it. If I can't take a little something like that, I don't need to be in this business."

Tige watched Ed as he threw a rag over his shoulder and walked off to serve two new customers. Then he looked timidly at Marvin who was staring down at him angrily.

"Ain't no San'a Claus, fo' real," he said, trying to defend himself. "That's what my mama told me."

"Your mother probably told you a lot of things, but one thing she obviously neglected to tell you about was good manners. You don't swear at people just because they ask you a simple question, and if you do, you apologize so you don't hurt their feelings. And when they give you things," Marvin nodded toward the half-eaten bag of potato chips in Tige's hands, "whether you want it or not, it's customary to say thank you, simply to show that you appreciate a little kindness when it's given to you."

Tige hung his head and toyed with a piece of a chip at the end of his fingers. Marvin was sounding like his mama when she was trying to tell him right from wrong. She'd talk to him about the evils of smoking, drinking, and dope. She told him that it would probably be different if he could afford such wasteful luxuries, but that he couldn't, so he might as well forget them. Such indulgences would only cause more trouble than they could possibly handle, and they certainly didn't need any more.

However, she had never mentioned anything about cursing. He had learned it from her, and it had no physical consequences except if he were to use it against her. And as far as good manners were concerned, he had never really learned any. The only things his mama had been insistent about were that he not give her any back talk, that he be nice and obedient to Carrie, and that he not mess with girls. By that, she meant no sexual contact. Girls get pregnant, she explained, and he could get VD.

The warning hadn't really been necessary for girls didn't interest him that much, sexually or otherwise. It may have been his age, he thought, that didn't let him see what Mojoe saw in halter-topped girls with bouncing bustlines and big thighs. To Tige, they simply looked trashy, like the prostitutes down on the corner who had been daily reminders of what his mama unwillingly had to go through to keep a roof over their heads. Girls were all right as long as they were girls, but when they began to act like women, that was where he drew the line. That was all the training Vanessa had tried to instill in him, and he'd sit and soak it in until she was through.

Marvin must have been through. He had silenced himself with a mouthful of scotch and water and was glaring ahead at the television set. Silence was his mama's next step. Supposedly she needed time to cool off. Supposedly Marvin needed time to cool off, too.

Tige watched the parade until it finally began to interest him again.

"I bet them majorettes freezin'," he said in an effort to nudge Marvin out of his presently grumpy mood. It didn't work, so he tried again later on.

"What makes all them thangs move like that? Them three li'l pigs keep stickin' they head out the window and they openin' and closin' they eyes. Is it somebody inside all of 'em makin' 'em move?"

"They're mechanical," Marvin explained, sounding slightly less grouchy. "They're all hooked up to move a certain way and I believe there's someone inside who's operating the whole thing."

"Is the one inside the one who built it?"

"I don't know. Maybe sometimes. I don't know."

"I thank they did a pretty good job whoever did it."

Marvin glanced over his shoulder at Tige, touched by his childlike attitude. It was truly easy to forget that he *was* a child—perhaps with a few grown-up traits, but nonetheless, still just a child.

Tige held up his potato chip bag as a final offering of peace. Marvin accepted and thanked him, then both allowed another hour of parade to pass before them.

The football game started at two-thirty. Tige didn't have that much knowledge of the game or its rules. What he liked was half time and watching the players run for touchdowns. He rooted for whichever team was in possession of the ball.

Marvin made a bet on the outcome of the game and also on a second game they watched afterward. The first one he won, which meant his bill had been taken care of. Tige attempted to sit still for the second game, but his stomach convinced him he was ready to leave.

"Hey, Marvin, when we gonna eat?"

"In a little while, when the game's over," Marvin told him.

"I'm hungry *now*."

"Tige, a few more minutes. Can't you see I'm busy?"

Marvin returned to his viewing and a sideline discussion with Ed and another interested customer, ignoring Tige completely.

By the time the game ended, the room had become busy and noisier, and Marvin was ten dollars richer. He looked around for Tige but saw no trace of him. He asked the bartender if he'd seen him.

"I think I saw him head out the door 'bout an hour ago."

"Okay, thanks."

Marvin stepped out into the chilly night air. His battered watch showed eight o'clock. He pondered which route his little friend might have taken. He was hungry, so he might have gone somewhere in search of food. Then again he may have just gone back to the apartment. *Or,* he may have gone his way, never to return. Marvin decided to search for a while on his way home, and if Tige didn't show up, that would just have to be that.

Marvin walked along the neon-lit streets until he heard Christmas carols being sung not far away. It occurred to him that Tige might have wanted to see the lighting of the giant Christmas tree, so he altered his course and took a three-block detour to Rich's. The two sections of the large department store were joined together two floors above the ground by an enclosed bridge, and anchored to the bridge was a seventy-foot Christmas tree. Hundreds of colored lights and ornaments sparkled brightly against a dark blue, starry background and the large glass windows were decorated to give a stained-glass effect. Glee clubs from eight different schools and organizations took turns singing Christmas carols, and almost nine-hundred people crowded the streets to witness the traditional lighting of the tree.

Sure enough, Marvin spotted Tige at the edge of the throng, perched atop a cement wall.

"It's beautiful, isn't it?" said Marvin.

"I ain't never seen it when it's all lit up," Tige said without taking his gaze from the dazzling star atop the tree. "Every time I was down heah, they never had it lit. It was always too light. Is that the biggest Christmas tree in the world?"

"Probably not. It should be pretty close though. You ever find anything to eat?"

"Yeah, a lady bought me a box of fried chicken."

"Really?"

"Well, sort of. She was too fat ta eat all that anyhow. I saved ya a piece and a roll."

Tige pulled a crushed chicken box from his pocket, and handed it to Marvin.

"Thank you very much," said Marvin, leaning against the high wall that Tige was sitting on.

"I wished I had a camera so I could take a picture of it. That's pretty. I bet they light bill gonna be somethin' though."

"Christmas comes but once a year," stated Marvin philosophically. "Some people make the most of it," he added.

As Marvin ate, Tige tried to sing along in a chorus of "Jingle Bells." After a loud and joyous round of "We Wish You a Merry Christmas," the crowd began to disperse slowly, and Marvin helped Tige down from the wall.

"Come on. It's too late to walk. Let's see if we can't catch a bus. Um, it's getting cold. Shouldn't you have a heavier coat?"

"Nawl, I ain't cold."

"You sure?"

"Uh huh."

"Well, suit yourself."

They walked for a block and stopped at an isolated bus stop.

"You sure you're not..." Marvin started to ask, but stopped when he saw how Tige was trembling and hugging himself to keep warm.

Marvin reached out and pulled Tige toward himself.

"Come here. You're about to freeze your rump off," he said, unbuttoning his fur-lined trench coat. He pulled

Tige flush against his body and rebuttoned the coat except for one button, which allowed Tige's face to stick out.

"Better?" he asked.

Tige glanced up at him, then without answering, he pulled his face in and turned around inside the coat. He nuzzled his face into Marvin's sweater and then remained still. Marvin fastened the last button and rested his arms across Tige's back for additional warmth.

The bus came fifteen minutes later. The warmth of the bus and Marvin's comfortable arm were an open invitation for a short nap.

"Up, up," Marvin nudged him. "Time to get off."

On the block-and-a-half walk to the apartment, Tige began to sing his version of "Jingle Bells," mumbling nearly all the words.

"If you want to sing it right, I'll be glad to teach you the words," Marvin offered.

"I'll sang it the way I wanna."

"But if you knew the words to it, you could sing it along with other people or something."

"I 'on't care. I 'on't wanna learn it."

"What have you got against learning the words to a song? Or do you simply dislike *any* form of education?"

Tige hummed his song, refusing to answer the question.

"That's it, isn't it? You just don't want to learn *anything*."

"I know anough already."

"You don't know the words to the song. I wouldn't be surprised if you couldn't even read that sign over there."

Marvin pointed to a cigarette billboard across the street. Tige glanced at it and looked away.

"I 'on't care."

"You should, you know. You really should. You need

an education, Tige. You need to find out what the world's about."

"I *already* know what the world's about!" Tige stopped in his tracks. "It's about all y'all white crackers! 'Specially the big ones. You 'on't halfway count 'cause you ain't that much no way. But I'm talkin' 'bout the ones that makes up all them laws sayin' you gotta have a edjacation. My mama was turned down over twen'y jobs just 'cause she didn't have that piece of gradjawaitin' paper whitey say fo' her ta have ta prove she learned the thangs whitey wanted her ta know."

"You're being a bit prejudicial. You know there are some blacks up there with whitey too."

"Yeah, but look how long it took 'em ta git dare. And whitey still pullin' the strangs."

"You're just jealous, that's all. You're just plain jealous because you don't have what some of the more fortunate have. There are poor whites as well as blacks and every other race you can think of. No one knows exactly how it happened or what to do about it, but if you want to be like your mother with no education and no hope for the future then you go right on the way you're going now."

Tige turned his back and walked on.

"That's your answer to things, isn't it? Let me ask you a question. Just what are you going to do when you grow up?"

"Who says I'll grow up? Who says I won't die tanight—ffsst, just like my mama."

"You shouldn't talk like that. Who's to say you won't live to be a hundred? It's just as much a possibility. What would you have to show for those years? A wife, family, a home and job. You can make it happen if you want to."

Tige stopped and turned before going up the stairs to the apartment. He looked at Marvin and huffed.

"Look who's talkin'. You been through all that crap and what you gotta show fo' it? A dump, a liquor bottle, and bad breath. Man, all that work you been through and you ain't got a damn thang. But I guess that's what the world needs though, mo'e well-edjacated drunks."

"Apologize!" Marvin demanded angrily.

"Fo' what? It's all true, ain't it?"

"That gives you no right to insult people. You should learn to have a little more respect. Respect others and they will respect you."

"Like hell, they will!"

Marvin lunged forward and grabbed Tige by his collar. Speaking through clenched teeth, he tried desperately to control his temper.

"Now, I've asked you not to curse, *repeatedly,* and I've asked you to try and act a little more like a human being. If you can't do those two simple things, then you take a walk, and I don't *ever* want to see your little black face again!"

Tige stared at him, frightened at first, but then angered by his demands.

"You git yo' hand off me."

Marvin released him and stood away.

"You know what else you can do too," Tige told him.

Marvin nodded. "Yeah, I know what I can do, but don't tempt me, son, please don't tempt me."

"Go ta hell, you bast—" Tige's sentence was cut short when a huge white hand suddenly slapped him across his face.

"You'd better go, little boy, while I'm still in a good mood."

Tige rubbed his face and stood to one side, out of Marvin's path. He felt like taking out his knife and stabbing him in the back. Marvin must have been reading his thoughts, for just as he reached for it, Marvin turned his head.

"Keep your hands in your pockets if you want to keep them at all. I don't feel like playing games."

Tige let the knife drop back into its place, then backed away slowly as Marvin stared and waited. Then he turned and ran.

Marvin switched on the radio and tried to relax. The little guy had finally gone too far. He thought he had been fair with the boy; there's only so much a person *can* take. He took a long swig from a bottle of scotch and decided not to let the matter upset him any further.

"Tonight's weather," the voice on the radio was saying, "is going to be a bit chilly with the temperature dipping into the lower teens. That's right, folks—winter is here. Time to get out the old firewood, bring in the plants, and sit back and relax while we play you some easy-listening music."

Marvin gulped down another swallow of scotch and spoke to himself aloud.

"He ought to freeze out there. Acts like it'd kill him to say one decent thing for a change. Let him find some other sucker to mooch off of—this pigeon's closed."

As far as Tige was concerned, *everything* was closed. He wished he'd known sooner that he wouldn't have a place to stay for the night—there were no choice spots in this neighborhood. Everything was either locked up securely or openly exposed to the wind and cold. He thought of hopping a bus and going downtown to sneak into one of the hotels. He decided that that was a good idea, but not knowing the bus schedule, he had no way of knowing that he had just gotten off the last bus going anywhere.

He stood beside the bus stop hopping from foot to foot and rubbing his legs together for warmth. His effort did little good, as the wind slapped against him and whirled up under his pantlegs. There had to be a better place to wait, so he started to walk. If it weren't so cold he could probably have walked to town, but his legs were beginning to ache and everything else was turning numb. He came to a third bus stop, one that had a bench behind it. He sat down, pulling his legs up under his jacket, and began a rhythmless rocking motion.

He wondered what Marvin was doing right now. He had really blown his chance for free room and board. He had liked Marvin, too, but now it was too late to prove it. So he rocked sleepily on the bench for more than an hour. Finally he realized that the bus was not coming, but he saw no sense in moving; there was no place else to go. The feeling of helplessness returned, and he felt the need to cry. He made up his mind to spend the night on the bench, and if he wasn't frozen to death by morning—which he much preferred at the moment—then he would return to Carrie for help and submit, if necessary, to the proper authorities. But for now, the bench would have to suffice. He lay down, tucking as much of himself as possible into the jacket and waited to see if tomorrow would come.

It took an hour and a half for Marvin to cool down enough to go search for Tige, and forty minutes more to find him on the desolate corner. To see him huddled under the skimpy jacket made him realize what a louse he'd been to kick him out into the cold.

"Now you know you can't spend the night out here," he said without getting a response. "Come on, Tige, you'll catch pneumonia." There was still no response. "Tige?"

He looked closer and saw the barely noticeable rise and fall of Tige's body as he breathed. He stooped over and pulled back the collar that hid Tige's face, and saw one wide, tearful eye as it looked back at him.

"I'll take you back," Marvin said softly, then pulled off his coat to wrap about Tige. He hurried home with the fifty-five-pound bundle and released him on the bed where he rubbed down his arms and legs to help get his circulation back to normal, then covered him with warm blankets. Tige slid beneath the blankets, head and all, and curled up tightly.

"I'll get you something hot to drink," said Marvin. "Get myself something to drink. Do you drink coffee? Or maybe I have some milk I could warm up. Let me see."

He rummaged through the refrigerator and came up with half a quart of milk.

"Ah, this should do it. It really is getting cold these days. Glad I decided to pay my gas bill this month."

He put the milk on to heat then returned to Tige's bedside. Except for an uncontrollable trembling, he seemed to have fallen asleep. Marvin looked down upon the small lump underneath the blankets.

"I'm sorry," he said softly. "I was just a little angry. I really didn't mean to hit you. It won't happen again. I realize now that it isn't your fault. You can't help what life's done to you. I suppose if I were you, I'd be the same way. . . . You want the milk now? It should be ready."

The head of the covers moved back and forth in a negative motion.

"All right then. If you should need anything, just . . . you know. Goodnight."

"I've got work to do today," said Marvin over breakfast. "You feel like earning a little money?"

"Doin' what?"

"Well, let's see."

Marvin leafed through a small brown tablet.

"Today's Friday. I've got a basement to clean out— it's full of old paint cans, newspapers, soda bottles, and who knows what else. Looked like a pretty good-sized job. Interested?"

"Git paid fo' it?" Tige questioned.

"Of course. Twenty-five dollars for the whole thing."

Tige thought it over and as there was no reason not to, he agreed.

"Okay. Do I git half?"

"Sure. If you can do half the work. Get a move on. We want to get an early start."

At the end of a long day, Tige dropped like a rock onto the bed as soon as he walked through the door.

"I'm dead," he announced.

"You are? The way you talked before, I thought you were used to a little hard work."

"*Hard* work? Man, that's chain gang work. Stoopin' over and pickin' up this, and draggin' all that junk, and all that carr'in' all the way to the street. Man, I'm so'e all over."

"You know the best thing for that, don't you?"

"What?"

"Soak yourself in a nice hot bath."

"*Bath?* I just had a bath Monday."

"That recent, huh? Take another one, you'll feel better—and smell better."

"Hey, what 'bout my money?" Tige asked, sitting up slowly.

"Your money . . . well, I'll tell you, Tige—I'm afraid I'll have to give that to you some other time. See, I don't have another job lined up until Tuesday, and tomorrow's grocery day. We're running pretty low on everything, so . . ."

"So you just gonna spend my money without even askin' me, huh?"

"Well, I didn't think you'd mind that much, considering you're getting free room and board."

"But that's still my money. You already owe me from yeste'day."

"You don't have to remind me; I know I owe you, but you want to eat tomorrow, don't you?"

"I can git my own food. You 'on't be takin' my money with that kinda deal."

"All right, if that's the way you want it. Here."

Marvin pulled out the money and counted off ten dollars.

"Your five-fifty worth of work and the four-fifty I borrowed. That's all of it, right?"

Tige looked at the bills and folded them in his fist.

"It's *my* money," he said defensively.

"I know it's yours. I suppose if I lived your life, I'd be holding on to every nickel and dime I got too. Let's just forget the whole thing. Go on and take your bath while I fry some eggs or something. Scoot."

Tige scooted off to the bathroom, then returned a few minutes later while the water was running in the tub.

"What I'm 'pose ta do—drip dry or pop in the toaster?"

"Oh, you need a towel?"

"Yeah. Or either a lotta toilet paper."

Marvin reached into a drawer and pulled out two blue towels.

"I see I'm going to have to get to the laundromat tomorrow too. Here you go. Hang the other up for me."

"You gonna take a bath too?"

"Uh huh."

"You got a rubber duck?"

"Rubber—what would I be doing with a rubber duck?"

"How should I know? I thought white folks always took baths with they li'l' rubber duckies," Tige grinned. Marvin chuckled lightly.

"Get going. Rubber duckie . . . crazy."

Tige started off, but forgetting something, he backtracked.

"Heah." He held out his money to Marvin. "You can keep it, but don't spend it till I tell ya to."

"As you wish, my lord."

Then Tige went off to bathe. After bombarding his washcloth with the soap for twenty minutes, he came into the kitchen with the towel wrapped around him, Tarzan-style.

"I ain't got nothin' clean ta sleep in."

"You *don't* have *anything* clean to sleep in," Marvin corrected him.

"I know. That's what I just said."

"Oh, well forgive my hearing. Look in that third drawer over there. I should have a couple of T-shirts left."

"Okay."

Tige rumbled through the drawer, found his intended nightgown and a pair of striped boxer shorts that he held up to examine.

"Hey, Marv."

"What?"

"You gotta be kiddin', man," he teased, dancing the shorts around by the elastic band. "You wear these thangs fo' real?"

"Put them back and mind your own business. Come on and eat before it gets cold."

Tige obeyed, dropping the shorts back into the drawer and slipping into Marvin's giant T-shirt. It fit like a tent, stopping at his calves and slipping off at the shoulders. He hung on to it and went to eat.

After dinner, Marvin took his turn in the bathtub. He came out dressed in a rumpled maroon bathrobe, showing off his pale, nearly hairless, but fairly muscular legs, and pulled on a pair of pajama bottoms.

"Ready for the lights to go out? I'm a little on the bushed side."

"I wanna heah a bedtime story."

"*Bedtime* story? You?"

"Yeah, why not? White kids git 'em, don't they? Ain't I good anough?"

"Okay, a short one. Get in bed."

Tige bounced on the bed and got under the covers. Marvin followed and lay alongside him.

"Okay, you're ready for the story?" he asked.

"Yeah."

"All right then, it goes like this. Once upon a time, there lived an elf in the beginning of this huge book. And one day he decided to make a journey to the back of the book to see how the other half of the world was living. So he traveled hard and long, and lo and behold, he got to the very last page, turned it over—and guess what it said."

"What?"

"The end. Goodnight."

"Aw, man, that wa'n't even good."

"I never said I was Mother Goose. Go to sleep."

Marvin turned on his side and switched off the lamp.

"Hey, Marv."

"What is it, Tige?"

"It's dark."

"Close your eyes, you won't be able to notice it."

"Oh," said Tige, and he closed his eyes and moved in closer to Marvin. He tried not to think about the darkness, but it didn't work. "Hey, Marv, you 'sleep?"

"I would like to be. What's wrong now?"

"It's still dark."

"It is? What about the light from the heater—isn't that enough?"

"It's spooky. I can see thangs."

"Tige, do you want me to turn the light back on?"

"If you wanna."

"I wanna, I wanna. Now, is that better? Go to sleep," Marvin grumbled, burying his face in the pillow and covering up his head to avoid the light. Tige was quiet for a few moments until he remembered something.

"Hey, Marv."

"*Hello*, Tige," Marvin's muffled voice came from beneath the covers.

"You 'sleep yet?" Tige asked him.

"What do you think?"

"Oh. I just wanted ta ask a question."

"Be brief."

"What?"

"I said, what is it?" Marvin raised his voice but not his head.

"Oh, well you said we gonna have ta go to the groc'ry sto'e and the wash house tamorrow, right?"

"Yes."

"What time you gonna go?"

"What time? I don't know—*some* time. Why?"

"I just wanted ta know if it was all right if I go downtown and watch the cartoons on television first."

Marvin perked up from beneath the blanket, surprised by Tige's thinking it necessary to ask his permission. He looked at him and saw that he was obviously waiting and hoping for a "yes" to his question.

"Sure. It's Saturday. You do anything you like. I'll take care of everything else, okay? Now get to sleep before I *put* you to sleep, and if I hear one more, 'Hey, Marv,' I'm going to pick you up by your Afro and toss you out on your rump. Is that clear enough?"

"Yeah."

"All right, goodnight."

"Night...Marv? Just kiddin'."

Saturday, Tige spent half the day watching television downtown. He turned the channels of four different TV sets to four different stations so he wouldn't miss any of his favorites that came on at the same time. He wondered if the salespeople around were getting tired of seeing his face. They'd look at him, but they never said anything. He supposed they figured he didn't have a set of his own to watch, so they just left him alone.

When he returned home—already he was thinking of it as home—he found the door locked. Marvin must have gone off to the store or the laundromat, he thought. So Tige went off in search of the nearest of each.

He found Marvin in the frozen food section of the grocery store.

"Hi. How'd you find me?" Marvin asked.

"I looked," Tige replied, as he looked into the cart to see what Marvin had gotten so far. "You been to the wash house yet?"

"Yes, I've already taken care of that."

"You wash any of my stuff?"

"I didn't know you wanted me to. But I did, just in case." Marvin picked up four different TV dinners and showed them to Tige. "Which one of these do you like?"

"Which one got food in 'em?"

Marvin put the four into the cart and gathered up six more. "I'm glad you're not picky about what you eat. My kids turned their noses up at everything."

Marvin strolled away from the frozen foods and Tige followed behind.

"You want me ta help?"

"If you like. You can go get two quarts of milk and a box of cornflakes for me. You like cornflakes, don't you?"

"Yeah, bedder'n that straw of yo's."

Marvin continued his shopping in the meat department, then wondered why it was taking so long for Tige to come back. He turned down one of the aisles just in time to catch Tige slipping a package under his jacket.

"Put it back," Marvin ordered in a low voice, startling him at first.

"Marvin, man you sked me. I thought you was somebody else."

"And I thought I sent you after some milk and cereal."

"I was gonna git 'em..."

"After you filled your pockets, I suppose."

"I was just tryin' ta help ya out."

"Help me some other way and put it all back."

"Back? I cain't; too many people 'round now, somebody might see me."

"Somebody's already seen you—me. And if I saw you, someone else could have just as easy."

"But if I start put'in' it back, somebody gonna catch me."

"No one will bother you as long as you don't try to walk out the door with anything. Now either put it in this basket or back where you got it from. We're not leaving here until you do one or the other."

Tige hesitated angrily, then sighed and began secretly unloading his jacket with Marvin following his every move.

"Is that all of it?" Marvin asked.

"Yeah."

"The truth?"

"I 'on't lie," Tige growled.

"All right then, I believe you. But a young man who doesn't lie shouldn't steal either. You may have done it before, but as long as you're staying under my roof, I don't expect it to happen again. Do I make myself clear?"

"Yeah, yeah."

"And another thing. We might not have much money between us, but what we've got, we'll use until we run out. Then we'll just go and earn us some more. Is that a deal?"

"*Deal?*" Tige walked off and picked up a box of crayons that he threw into the buggy. "Yeah."

For the rest of the afternoon, Tige watched wrestling and roller derby with Marvin on Ed's television set until he tired of the stuffiness of the place and decided to leave.

[80]] *Frankcina Glass*

Marvin returned home some time later, a bit tipsy. He found Tige sitting cross-legged on the bed with his coloring book and new crayons. Marvin growled like a crazed bear and grabbed Tige under his arms, threw him into the air twice, then dumped him back onto the bed.

"Hey, man! You crazy when you drunk, ain't cha?"

"I am *not* drunk," Marvin replied lightheartedly as he struggled out of his coat. "I *never* get drunk. Ever!"

"Oh. You just go crazy by yo'self then, huh?"

Marvin flopped down on his side of the bed, slurred an incomprehensible response, then began leading the orchestra on the radio in a version of "A Summer Place." He was asleep before the song ended. Tige pulled off his shoes for him, covered him up, and went back to his coloring.

Sunday looked as though it would be terribly dull. It was rainy and dreary, which only meant that the weather would get colder afterward. There seemed to be nothing to look forward to until Marvin finally crawled out of bed and pretended not to have a hangover. Then he scrambled around in his closet for a while and came out with a one-thousand-piece jigsaw puzzle for them to work on.

"I don't know how many times I've started putting this thing together, then I'd lose interest, and put it back up."

"What's it a picture of?" Tige asked.

"See?" Marvin showed him the picture on the box.

"Is that somethin' special?"

"Yes, it's the Leaning Tower of Pisa."

"The *what* of pizza?"

"Not pizza—Pisa. See, it's a tower and it's leaning and

it's in Pisa, Italy. You *have* heard of Italy, haven't you?"

"Yeah, in the movies. That's a real place?"

"Of course it's a real place."

"You ever been dare?"

"As a matter of fact, I have."

"When?"

"Years ago, when I was small. I went with my parents on a vacation."

"Where is Italy, and how did y'all git dare?"

"Italy's in Europe, and Europe is a continent across the ocean. We went there on an ocean liner."

"Oh, you mean a boat?"

"I'd hardly call it a boat. It was a ship, you know, with a swimming pool aboard, private rooms—sort of like a hotel on water."

"Yeah, I know what you talkin' 'bout now. Those thangs sank though."

"Luckily, I was never on the ones that did that."

"What other places you done been?"

"A few others, but you don't really want to hear about them."

"How you know I 'on't wanna heah 'bout 'em? I asked, didn't I? Shit, the only..." Tige looked up and found that Marvin had made note of the word and decided to let it pass.

"The only places I ever been," he continued, "was places I could git ta on the bus, and not even all *them*. I ain't even been ta Stone Mountain yet, or Six Flags Over Georgia, or nothin'. So you can tell me the places you been, and if I 'on't ever git ta go ta 'em, least I'll know about 'em."

"Okay. If you really want."

Marvin found himself telling stories he never thought

he'd get a chance to tell anyone. It felt good to him to have someone around, even if it *was* just a little black kid with a mountain-load of questions.

After a few hours—and not much accomplished on the puzzle—Marvin took a break for a pick-me-up. He sat back at the table with his bottle and a jelly glass.

Tige watched him as he poured himself a drink and took a sip. "What 'bout me?" he asked.

"What about you, what?"

"I want somethin' ta drank too."

"Well, you can get yourself some milk or something."

"I want some of that," Tige nodded toward the liquor.

"This?" Marvin grinned. "No, you don't want any of this. Stuff's poison—rot your liver out."

"Ain't it rot'in' yo' liver out?"

"My liver's old anyway. Why don't you get yourself some milk if you're thirsty."

"Is you thirsty?"

"What?"

"I said, is you thirsty? You drankin' that stuff 'cause you thirsty or just 'cause you like ta git drunk?"

"I am not drinking to get drunk."

"Den why? If you was just thirsty, you could drank some water. So why you drank that stuff fo'?"

"I drink it because . . . well, because it's just a nasty habit I've gotten myself into. And it's one you're better off not getting into.

"Uh huh. Well, cain't I make my own decision 'bout that?"

"Tige, I'm serious. There are enough juvenile alcoholics running around already without me helping to create another one."

"Oh. You mean it's all right ta be a drunk grown-up but not a drunk kid."

"I mean, you should be old enough to make a sensible decision."

"Uh huh. And how old was you when ya made yo' sensible decision?"

"Don't be such a..."

Marvin nodded his head. "Okay," he said. "Sure, why not."

He got up and got another glass, which he filled to its halfway mark and placed in front of Tige.

"There you go. Shouldn't take that much for you."

He sat down again and waited for Tige to pick up his glass. He clicked it with his and smiled.

"Cheers," he said, then gulped down the remainder of his drink and sat back to watch Tige with his.

Tige sniffed at it and whirled it around in the glass before finally bringing it to his lips and taking a mouthful.

It almost never made it past his tongue. He scowled and started to spit it back into the glass, but he saw how slyly Marvin was watching him, so he decided to swallow—*anything* to get it out of his mouth. It burned his tongue, his throat, and the bottom of his stomach where it landed. He tried hard to keep from coughing and found Marvin holding onto his forehead and snickering.

"That stuff tastes bad! How can people sit and drank that stuff?"

"You're just not used to it. Take another swallow."

"Ain't! That stuff tastes terrible! I 'on't even see how you can drank it."

"Rarely does one drink for mere taste alone. Some people hate the taste, but they still do it."

"Fo' what? What's the reason?"

"Different people drink for different reasons."

"Well, what's yo' reason?—or do you got any?"

"Yes, I have reasons. I think everyone has. Sometimes I drink to get high, I guess. You know—get a little happy feeling going to relax or calm my nerves. Then there are times when you'd like to forget things, sort of block them out. And you can tune out reality if something's bothering you. Sometimes you just need a little extra courage . . . or a friend. I—I suppose I've used everyone of those excuses at one time or other. My only excuse now is that it's just a habit. I don't feel I have to drink—I don't need to. . . . I just don't have a good enough reason to stop, I guess." He fell silent, feeling suddenly ashamed. He looked at Tige with a pained expression.

"Listen to the mouth of experience. I spend good money on bad booze, to get drunk and feel rotten and all for what? All for a stupid habit."

"You a alcoholic, ain't cha?" Tige asked.

Marvin shook his head. "No, I don't think so. Then sometimes, I'm not so sure."

Tige lifted his glass and handed it to Marvin.

"Drank the rest of that."

"Why?"

"I want you to. Drank it."

Marvin stared at the clear, smelly liquid for a few seconds, then poured it with a steady hand back into the bottle and recapped it.

"Mmh. I've never done that before. Felt rather nice."

"Shows you ain't no reg'lar drunk."

"Yeah."

"Marv, if you want me to, I'll help ya quit."

"Only alcoholics need help to quit. So—just keep reminding me that I'm not one, okay?"

"Okay."

Marvin stuck the bottle back into the drawer and settled back down with Tige to continue work on the puzzle.

On their way to a job in West End, Tige temporarily lost contact with Marvin when he stopped to watch some schoolchildren at recess on the school's playground. Some were playing kickball, others were sliding down slides, swinging on swings, and getting dizzy on the merry-go-round. Tige wandered around the school building, able to look up into the windows and see classes going on. A little girl happened by one of the windows, saw him, and waved. He waved back and she disappeared. It had been such a long time since he'd been to school that he had nearly forgotten what it was like.

Finally he managed to pull himself away, and as he turned around, he confronted a dark blue uniform and a silver badge. His first instinct was to run, but unfortunately he couldn't move fast enough. A strong, dark hand grasped him by the arm and held him tight.

"No you don't," the officer said. "Shouldn't you be in there instead of out here? What's yo' name?"

Tige didn't attempt to answer either of his questions. This was the first time he had ever been caught by the police for anything, and he was scared stiff.

"I asked you a question: why ain't you in school? You playin' hooky? What's yo' name? Why ain't you in school, boy?"

"Excuse me," Marvin appeared from nowhere to the rescue. "I believe I can answer all of that for you," he said, as he took Tige's free hand. The officer released Tige's other arm and stepped back for the explanation.

"How do you do," Marvin went on with unquestionable charm. "I'm Harold Gibbs, and this is Eric Michaels. We were separated for just a little while there..."

"What's he doin' out of school, *if* he goes at all."

"You're right, he doesn't attend school. He has a perfectly good reason, though."

"I'd like to hear it," said the officer with his arms folded in front of him.

"Well, Eric has a problem. See, he's a bit... *disturbed*," Marvin nearly whispered it to the man, over Tige's head.

"See, his father was a very brutal man—mistreated him a great deal until the neighbors thought they should report him. Only by then, they were a bit late as far as the boy was concerned. Scarred him terribly. I doubt seriously if he even understood a word you said. He won't even answer to his own name nowadays. Watch. Eric. Eric?"

Tige took the simple hint Marvin gave him and kept his eyes on the sidewalk and his mouth closed.

"See what I mean?"

"Oh... I'm sorry," the cop apologized. "I didn't know. You know, I was wonderin' why he couldn't open his mouth. I'm sorry if I scared him. Are you his doctor or somethin'?"

"No, I'm not. I'm just a volunteer worker. I take him

for walks, play with him, be his friend, that sort of thing. It's really very rewarding to be able to help people like him ..."

Tige pulled on his hand and grunted.

"Oh, I think he may have to use the bathroom. It's been nice talking to you but you will excuse us, won't you? Goodbye."

Marvin put his arm around Tige's shoulders and walked him away.

"Thought you said you wa'n't no con man," Tige spoke, once they had gotten far enough away.

"Necessity is the mother of invention."

"Huh?"

"I said, you'd be in trouble if I *hadn't* thought of something."

"Oh."

"And, Tige, if I were you, next time I wouldn't stand that close to a school, unless of course you're on the *inside* and not the out. Although that is where you should be."

"Yeah, yeah, I know, I know."

"Oh, don't worry. I won't try to force you to go to school. It'd be a bit awkward the way things are at the moment anyway. But it's your life—do with it as you wish."

Marvin awoke the next morning disappointed to find that Tige was gone. His first thought was that perhaps his little friend had decided it was time to split, but when he looked around, he saw that Tige's clothes had been left behind. No matter where the boy had gone, it wasn't for good.

Marvin went to work alone and returned home the same way. He was just about to worry that Tige might not come back when the door opened behind him and in walked his worry.

"Where have you been all day?" Marvin asked.

"Where you thank?"

"If I could think of where, I wouldn't ask."

"I been ta school," Tige answered matter-of-factly.

"School?"

"Yeah. You know one of them buildin's with the teachers and the books..."

"I know what a school is. And you went there."

"Yeah. Well, you been holl'in' 'bout me learnin' somethin', ain't cha?"

"So you just went out and went to school for one day."

"Yep."

"Well? Did anyone say anything to you—the teachers or someone?"

"Yeah, a couple asked who I was and was I 'pose ta be in they class."

"And what did you tell them?"

"I told 'em I was visitin'; that I just moved to Atlan'a and I was checkin' out all the schools ta see which one I wanted ta go to."

"Don't tell me they believed that?"

"Well, see, they 'on't know me like you, so they *had* to."

"Uh huh. So tell me, what did you do today in school? Learn anything?"

"Yeah, I learnt somethin'. In one class, they was showin' a film 'bout 'lectricity and Benjamin—uh, what's that dude's name?"

"Franklin?"

"Yeah, him. Anyway, it was a cartoon film showin' how 'lectricity works and where it comes from and that bald-headed guy with hair was catchin' lightnin' with his kite. Hey, you ever heah the sayin' 'bout lightnin' don't strike the same place twice?"

"Yes, I've heard it."

"You know why that is?"

"No, I don't believe I remember. Maybe it has something to do with the atmosphere or the position of the clouds..."

Tige puckered his lips and shook his head.

"No? Then why doesn't lightning ever strike the same place twice, Einstein?"

"'Cause," Tige replied, "when it strikes a place the first time, that place ain't dare no mo'e." He chuckled quickly and changed the subject.

"I ate lunch too. We had some hamburger paddies, some mashed potatoes, some turnip greens, some co'nbread, some peanut budder cookies, and some cold milk."

"Did you pay for your lunch?" Marvin asked.

"Nope. But I didn't steal it neither. I told the teacher I didn't have no money fo' lunch, so she bought it fo' me."

"That was nice of her. See, it pays to be honest."

"Sometimes. Anyway, I saved you a coupla cookies. They pretty good."

Tige reached into his pocket and brought out the cookies wrapped in a paper napkin. Then he withdrew from his lining two slightly thick paperback schoolbooks.

"I got dese books so you can start teachin' me somethin'."

"Me? You want *me* to teach you?"

"Yeah. You smart and all."

"Yes, but I'm no teacher."

"Aw, Marv, come on. You know I cain't go ta school. They gonna be tryin' ta find out where I come from and try ta stick me in a home. Come on, man-n-n."

Marvin heaved a sigh and surrendered. He picked up the books and leafed through them.

"You didn't take these from another kid, did you?"

"Nawl, I swiped 'em—I mean *borrowed* 'em from the liberry."

"Yeah, I bet. And it's li*brary*, not liberry."

"Li*brary*. See, I'm learnin' already. Come on, let's git started."

Tige pulled off his coat and took a seat at the table. Marvin pulled up a chair next to him.

"Which one we gonna do first?" Tige asked.

"Well, let's see what we have. One's English, the other's math."

"Math is 'rithmetic, ain't it?"

"Yes it is."

"One's 'rithmetic and one's English," Tige decided over the two. "Damn, that ain't much of a choice," he grumbled, then felt Marvin's cold stare on him.

"Oh, that just slipped a li'l', you know."

"I know. We'll start with the English book. You wouldn't happen to know what an interjection is?"

"That's when you git a needle in yo' arm," answered Tige, moving his hand from his behind to rest on his forearm.

"It seems," said Marvin, "that your major problem—among other things—is with interjections. Those are words you feel you have to say before saying anything else. For instance, what's the first thing you'd say if you stubbed your toe?"

"I 'on't know. Maybe damn, shit, or . . ."

"Ah, that's quite sufficient, thank you. Now see, that's your problem. What you need to do is add a few synonyms to your vocabulary."

"Run that by me ag'in?"

"Synonyms. Synonyms are words that are spelled differently, pronounced differently, but carry the same meaning. For example, let's take the word 'damn.' A good substitute for that would be 'darn.' It means the same thing, only it doesn't sound as vulgar. And the other word you used; a good substitute for that would be, 'shoot.' I admit it doesn't mean the same, but it's good for stubbing toes. And one more while we're at it—'hell.' In place of that, you could use, 'heck.'"

"Go ta heck? That 'on't sound right."

"Good. At least it should keep you from giving out directions."

"Well, open the book and just learn me ta read."

"Just how far along in reading are you?"

"I 'on't know."

Marvin opened the book in front of him and pointed to a sentence.

"Can you read that?"

"That's a 'one' right dare, and that's a 'A' ... and that word look like 'is.' I 'on't thank I can read the rest of it."

"The *rest* of it? You haven't read *any* yet. An 'A' and and a 'one' is not reading."

"I told ya I couldn't read ta start with."

"Well, what exactly have you learned in school so far? Do you know your alphabet—your ABC's?"

"Yeah, I know 'em some."

"Say them."

"A-b-c-d-e-f-g...g...let me thank—what comes after g? P-q...nawl, that ain't right—is it?" Tige asked in confusion.

"You don't know them. Do you know your numbers?"

Tige stared down at the book.

"I know 'em," he said, trying not to seem too ignorant. "But I git mixed up with 'em sometimes."

"Oh, that's just great!" Marvin grunted snobbishly.

"Well, I never said I was no genius."

"You didn't say you were a complete moron, either!" Marvin snapped. "You should have at least stayed in school long enough to learn *that* much."

"I told you why I couldn't go ta school. I had ta work."

"Yes, of course. So what do you expect from me—a miracle? You expect to look at these books a couple of weeks and presto, you're literate?"

Tige slashed his hand out, knocking the books off the table.

"Man, I cain't do nothin' ta please you, can I? You git on my case 'cause I *don't* wanna learn, and you git on me 'cause I *do!* What all you want outta me?"

"What do *I* want? You mean you're doing this for me? Because if you are, you're wasting your time. You think it matters to me one way or the other if you grow up ignorant? Don't go out and grab a book and try to understand anything in it for my benefit. It doesn't do a thing for me if you do or don't. If you want to learn something, let it be for yourself. You're the one who's affected by it, not me."

"Aw, man, dump it!" Tige growled. "Fa'git it. Just fa'git the whole thang."

He got up and started to leave.

"Come back here and sit down."

"Fo' what? So you can holla at me some mo'e?"

"You sit your tail back in that chair. *Sit down* before I *knock* you down!" Marvin threatened, looking as though he meant it. Tige avoided his eyes and obeyed reluctantly.

"Now, you were saying you wanted to learn something."

"Nawl, I changed my mind."

"Why, all of a sudden?"

"That's my business."

"I asked you a question. Why'd you change your mind?"

Tige delayed in answering; then, while staring into his lap, he spoke.

"'Cause you try ta be funny," he started. "Somebody ask ya ta do 'em a favor and you sit and call 'em names and holla at 'em like they ain't got no feelin's."

He finished simply what he had to say. It was enough to make Marvin feel ashamed.

"I—I guess you can really tell it now, that I'm not much with children. I'm—I'm sorry.... But, Tige, don't you know that, still, when you want something bad enough, you don't let what others say or do turn you against it?"

"Man-n-n," Tige raised his head. "I wanted ta learn somethin'—*anythang*. I wanna be able ta at least write my name and read a li'l' so I can understand some thangs and be like other people. But the way you holla at folks, it's anough ta scare *anybody* outta doin' what they wanted to." He let his head droop back down toward his lap.

Marvin watched for a moment, then got up and retrieved a small writing tablet and a pencil from a drawer, wrote something on the tablet, and laid it in front of Tige. Tige studied it a second and looked at him.

"What's it say?"

Marvin took the pencil and pointed out the words.

"It says—to the best of my knowledge—Tige Jackson. Here." He handed him the pencil. "Practice it while I warm up something for dinner.

Marvin opened a can of spaghetti and meatballs and put them on to heat. Then he picked up the books that Tige had knocked on the floor. He laid on the bed to study them while Tige found contentment in working to master the delicate block letters of his name.

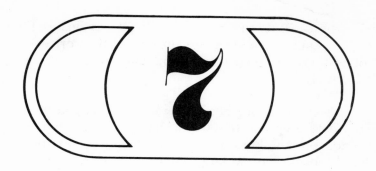

Christmas is such a depressing time of year when one is not prepared for it with no way *to* prepare for it. The day before Christmas was just another workday for Marvin and Tige. They were working cheaply, helping other people get ready for Christmas. They accepted a job stringing lights around the roof and windows of a house, and on another house they helped a clumsy Santa and two of his reindeer get up to the rooftop. They finished up the day pocketing only ten dollars.

"Ten tiny little dollars," Marvin sighed as they headed downtown to window shop before going home. "Barely enough to finish paying the rent. That's, of course, if we don't mind not eating for a few days."

"We fallin' behind, ain't we?" Tige asked.

"I wouldn't worry about it. If things get *too* tight, I've got a little something stashed in the bank I can draw on."

"How much in the bank?"

"That's none of your business."

"Just askin', just askin'. Man, I bet a lotta people gonna be downtown tanight."

"Last-minute shopping. Actually, this is the best time to buy. Quite a few stores will be cutting their prices on a lot of things to keep from being stuck with them after Christmas."

"My, my . . . look at that."

Tige was gazing at a young lady standing at the bus stop on the corner. She was a slender model-type, with golden brown skin and jet-black hair that was pulled tightly back into a large bun. As far as Tige was concerned, she was gorgeous!

The look he was giving her caught her eye as he and Marvin came nearer. Her responding eye contact was enough to encourage him to speak. He reached inwardly and brought forth all his charming knowhow.

"Hey dare, sweet thang," he beamed at her.

"Hello," she responded in a sweet, low, and sexy voice, sounding every bit like a goddess from heaven. She smiled at him and turned her head to throw a little wave as he passed her. Tige walked backward, grinning from ear to ear.

"Watch where you're . . ." Marvin tried to warn him, but it was too late. As Tige turned to face his original direction, he thumped into a sign post.

Marvin spit out a laugh and shook his head.

"When you get interested in women, you really get interested, don't you?"

"I ain't int'rested. I just thought she was kinda cute. Didn't you thank she was cute?"

"Yes, I thought she was very lovely."

"Well you sho 'on't act like it."

"I don't have to run into sign posts to show that I appreciate beauty. You didn't hurt yourself, did you?"

"Nawl—but I 'on't mean just beauty; I mean—well don't you like gulls just 'cause they gulls?"

"Girls, not gulls. Gulls are birds—and what do you mean, don't I like them? Of course, I like them. Where would the world be without them?"

"I was just askin', 'cause you 'on't act like you like 'em. You 'on't never try and pick none up or nothin'. You ain't a fag, is you?"

"Just because I don't go around picking up girls doesn't mean I make it a practice to go around picking up guys."

"I'm a guy—you picked *me* up."

"We're all entitled to our mistakes."

"Hey, look!" pointed Tige to another attractive young lady on the opposite side of the street. "Dare go another one."

"Don't point—it isn't polite. Why all of a sudden are you so interested in women anyway?"

"Bedder'n lookin' at you all the time. Hey, Marv."

"What?"

"You gonna ever git married ag'in? You know you ain't gonna find a wife the way you goin'."

"Who says I'm interested in finding a wife?"

"Dude yo' age oughtta want one. You ain't git'in' no younger. Don't you want a li'l' old broad ta keep you comp'ny in yo' old age?"

"No, and I wish you'd change the subject."

"Why?"

"Because I'd rather not discuss the matter."

"Why? I disgust madders to *you*. You can talk ta me about thangs, too."

"I'd rather not."

"How come? I just asked you a simple question. What you got 'gainst women? What's the madder, ain't you po'ent no mo'e?"

"Shut your *filthy* mouth!" Marvin snapped.

.⌐, I didn't mean nothin' by it. I was just jokin'."

⌐ell, you have a disgusting sense of humor and if
. have any more like that, keep them to yourself and
⌐⌐op pestering me."

Tige stopped in his tracks and pouted angrily.

"I *said* I was *sorry*. You say thangs ta me I 'on't like
sometimes."

Marvin walked on, ignoring him. Tige ran up behind
and continued to state his protest.

"Now see, how come you can say anythang you want
ta me and I have ta sit and listen, but when I say somethin'
ta you, you walk on like I ain't said a word?"

Marvin still didn't respond, so Tige ran in front of him
and faced him with his hands on his hips.

"Hey! Ain't I somebody too?"

Marvin looked down on him calmly, holding his
temper.

"Yes, you are somebody, and you do have the right to
ask any questions you like. But I'm somebody too, and I
have the right not to answer them. . . . Is there anything
else you'd care to discuss?"

Tige pouted and stepped to the side so Marvin could
take the lead. There was no use in pursuing the issue any
further.

By the time they reached the downtown district, both
their tempers had cooled and they were content to spend
the last of the daylight hours in the stores. Marvin's
favorite section was the stereo and record department.
Tige's favorite was the toy department. He'd look at every
box and package on the shelves, having a special fancy for
things on wheels. Marvin noticed how hesitant he was
about touching anything, as if he was afraid he'd break it
and have to pay for it. But when something was out of its
package and on the floor, he would take advantage for a
few moments, then leave it as he found it.

"Ready to go?" Marvin asked.

"Yeah. We gonna ride the bus or walk?"

"Unless you've got some loose change I don't know about, you'd better plan on walking. Let's get a move on before it gets pitch dark."

They walked silently through the streets and watched the people bustling about, carrying shopping bags full of toys and gifts. All seemed to be happy to have gotten their Christmas shopping completed.

"Hey, Marv." Tige stopped in front of a corner store that had bicycles as the main attraction in a window display. Marvin scanned the golden ten-speed bike in the window that Tige seemed fascinated by.

"Nice bike. I remember I bought my son one once. Spent a hundred-thirty-five dollars on the thing. Rode it for two weeks before he left it in somebody's driveway and it got run over. Had the nerve to ask for another one. Humph."

Marvin started to walk away but stopped when he noticed that Tige's eyes were still glued to the bike. He went back and stood behind him, watching in silence the reflection of Tige's face in the window. The boy seemed pitifully sad and hopeless—like those children whose pictures are flashed on the television screen so that people will send money to help save them. Marvin reached out and rubbed his hand on Tige's shoulder.

"How much you suppose it costs?" he asked.

"It used ta be a hundred dollars. It's been reduced ta nine'y-nine, nine'y-nine."

"Have you ever had a bicycle before?"

"I made me one, one time. When somebody else's bicycle got to'e up and they threw it away. I picked out what I could use till I had anough fo' a whole one. Mama never could affo'd ta buy me nothin'. She didn't like git'in' in debt. She never liked owin' people fo' thangs.

The times she did have money ta buy me somethin' fo' Christmas, she'd just spend it ta buy me shoes and clothes."

"What did you get last Christmas?" Marvin asked.

Tige sighed and shook his head. He pulled himself away from the window and walked on. Marvin watched him a second, then looked at the bike again. He patted the ten dollars in his pocket and ran some figures through his brain, coming up with a very disheartening total. He left the window and caught up with Tige.

"What kept ya?"

"Nothing. I was just looking at something. Say, Tige, how would you like to have that bicycle?"

Tige looked at him wonderingly.

"I'll get it for you," said Marvin.

"How?"

"How do you get things *you* can't pay for?"

Tige shook his head disapprovingly.

"Why not? *You* do it."

"I do it ta survive! I 'on't steal fo' fun. You steal somethin' like that and git caught, you go ta jail."

"What if I don't get caught?"

"Then don't 'spect ta try and give it ta me. You cain't eat a bicycle and you cain't wear it. I been goin' this long without thangs like that and I can *keep* goin'. You ain't gotta steal fo' me, Marv. It ain't yo' style and it ain't worth it."

Marvin was silent for a moment.

"Can I buy it for you? I could maybe put five dollars down on it and pay the rest by the month.

"That's still a lotta money, Marv. You already owe on the rent."

"I'll get a job."

"Aw, stop lyin', Marvin! You ain't never gonna work

and you know it. You'll just git yo'self in a lotta debt fo'
nothin'. Christmas is fo' them that got. I know a jolly, fat
white man ain't gonna come down my chimney and give
me nothin', so I 'on't 'spect it ta happen. I 'on't care 'bout it
no mo'e.... Come on, let's go home."

Marvin followed behind him, imagining how Tige
must have walked the streets in past Christmas seasons to
stare and mope at other children who had been luckier
than he was. How many times had he hoped for a miracle
and awoke to find it never came? And how many times
had he cried himself to sleep because of it?

When they were nearly home, Marvin stopped
alongside a rather full evergreen bush.

"Tige."

"What?"

"You still have your knife with you?"

"Yeah. Why?"

"Let me borrow it a minute. I want to get us a
Christmas tree."

"That ain't no Christmas tree," Tige frowned.

"A tree is just a tree. You have to add the Christmas to
it yourself."

Marvin took the knife and carved off about two feet
worth of tree. He held it up for Tige's approval.

"What do you think?"

"It's stupid.... I guess it'll do."

Marvin built a stand for the tree and centered it on top
of the table.

"Now, what'll we do for decoration?" he pondered
aloud.

"'Luminum foil," Tige suggested. "We can cut up
some ca'dboa'd in the shape of stars and thangs and cover
'em up with 'luminum foil."

"Brilliant idea, Holmes," Marvin agreed.

Using nearly a complete roll, they managed to decorate the tree with thin strands of shimmering foil and misshapened stars and balls.

"I 'on't know," Tige mused undecidedly. "I thank it needs somethin'."

"I think you're right. Any more ideas?"

"Needs some mo'e color or somethin'."

Tige was struck with an idea. He jumped from his chair to go get the playing cards.

"Cards? On a Christmas tree?"

"Why not?"

"Why not."

The cards were applied to the tree, with some dangling from thread while others sat on and in-between branches.

"It may not be the best decorating job I've ever seen, but it's certainly the most original one."

"I thank it looks kinda cute. I wish we had some way to light it up though."

Marvin snapped his fingers. "I've got it!" he exclaimed and proceeded to balance a flashlight from strings tied to the light socket above. He switched it on and turned off the room light. They sat and stared at the sparkling tinsel that dangled from the tree, catching and reflecting the small light from above, and also the unexpectant light from the fire of the living room heater.

"Gawd! That looks real good now. . . . Hey, Marvin?"

"Yes?"

"What was Christmas like in yo' days?"

"Oh, you mean back in the 1800s?"

"Yeah, back then. Was you po'?"

"No, I wasn't poor. My family was well off—not ecstatically rich, but we had a nice home with an upstairs and downstairs, two cars at all times, and even a housekeeper. It was nice. It was very nice."

"You always git what you wanted fo' Christmas?"

"I don't remember ever being disappointed on Christmas day. But with *my* family, it wasn't just receivng gifts that made us happy—it was the chance to get all the relatives together. My mother and grandmother would get in that kitchen and cook and bake up a storm—pies and cakes, coming and going. There'd be about thirty or forty uncles and aunts and cousins, and we'd toast marshmallows, drink eggnog, and then we'd all gather around the piano and sing carols. They'd always talk my sister and me into doing a duet."

"You had a sister?"

"Had one? No, I still have one, I think."

"What you mean, you thank? Don't ya know if ya got one or not?"

"I just haven't heard from her in a long time, that's all. She married and went to live in London. I used to get cards and letters from her all the time, but then I stopped answering them."

"How come? You 'on't like her no mo'e?"

"No, nothing like that. It just happened to be at the time when . . . when my wife died."

Marvin breathed in deeply and fingered the worn wedding band on his finger.

"I sort of lost touch with everyone back then. Catheryn—my wife—was a very beautiful lady. Had the loveliest green eyes. I met her when I was fourteen and fell in love the same day. We dated all through high school, and then we were married. Beautiful wedding. She wore white. Not too many women can wear white these days. But there she was in that long, flowing silken gown, like an angel she looked."

He paused a moment with a strange smile on his face. Tige stared at him intently, waiting impatiently for his next words.

"So long ago," Marvin sighed. "Twenty years together, then..." The smile on his face faded completely.

"How do you tell someone they're dying? It's not easy to look them straight in the eyes and tell them their life's just been canceled. That's one thing I never envy doctors. But Cathy took it pretty well. She said, 'Why sit and pout over it? We might as well be happy for the time we've spent and enjoy the time we have left.' She was brave. All the way to the final moment."

Tige saw a glittering in Marvin's eyes that shouldn't have been there. He seemed to be very deep within himself, oblivious to everything except what he was thinking.

"When she went—it was like the end of the world. I thought I'd..."

"Hey, Marvin, that's all right. You ain't gotta tell me no mo'e."

Knowing he hadn't yet gotten through to him, Tige reached out and patted the back of Marvin's hand to get his attention.

"Hey, Marv. Don't say no mo'e, man."

"What?" Marvin said, still not quite hearing what was being said. Then he blinked his eyes and looked in Tige's general direction. "What?"

"You 'memb'rin too much," Tige told him.

"Sometimes...sometimes memories are all that's left."

"Yeah, but you 'pose ta 'member the good stuff, not all the bad. And sometimes it's good ta try and fa'git some thangs. That's what I had ta do. I know you have ta cry some, but you 'pose ta git over it."

Marvin shook his head while staring ahead at the Christmas tree. "You don't understand, Tige. Some things can't be explained."

"Nawl, I understand all right. You still cryin' 'bout somebody's been dead fo' years; that's what I *don't* understand. You 'on't see me still yellin' over my mama, and it ain't hardly been a month. And don't thank I didn't love her neither."

Marvin stroked his temples as if they were in pain.

"Do me a favor, Tige, just go on to bed."

"Man, I'm tryin' ta tell ya somethin' . . ."

Marvin crashed his fist down on the table, shaking some of the ornaments down from the tree. Tige jumped up, wide-eyed.

"I told you to go to bed!" Marvin shouted in a hideous tone.

Tige moved slowly from the table, backing away in fear. Marvin watched him, anger still chiseled boldly into his features. Tige kicked off his shoes and slid under the covers, fully clothed.

Marvin got up in search of a drink. He downed a couple of ounces that were left in his last bottle, then grabbed his coat from the closet.

"Marvin, where you goin'?"

"None of your business—out!"

"Hey, Marvin, I'm sorry. When you comin' back?"

"When I'm good and ready!" he shouted and slammed the door.

Tige ran to the window to see which direction he had taken. More than likely he would head for his favorite bar. Tige returned to the tree and restored it to its original state. It had started out to be such a nice Christmas Eve, but now it had all gone sour, all because of someone who no longer existed except in Marvin's mind. It was easy to see now why Marvin wasn't interested in other women. That was a shame, but there was nothing to be done about it.

Tige peeled off his clothes, got back into bed, and switched on the radio to keep himself company. He thought he'd be able to stay awake until Marvin returned, but Nat King Cole's soothing voice lulled him to sleep with "The Christmas Song."

Morning came, and Tige awoke with a relieved feeling as
he found Marvin asleep beside him. There was no
indication of how he'd be once he was awake, but the
important matter was simply that he'd returned.

Tige sprang from the bed and jumped into his clothes
and shoes. He went into the bathroom to wash the sleep
from his eyes and, while he was at it—the rest of his face
also.

It irked him that in all the bathrooms he'd been in, no
one had ever bothered to lower the cabinet mirrors to
cater to short folks. Maybe he wasn't allowed to see
himself until he was four-feet-eight, which at the rate he
was growing, wouldn't be for another two or three years.

He stood up on the edge of the bathtub to admire
himself a few moments. He studied his wide, saucerlike
eyes. Women had always adored the huge, round, dark
globes. It was easy to see that he didn't get them from his
mama. But then, she wouldn't admit he had inherited
them from his father either. Tige didn't look anything like
Vanessa. Her eyes were smaller, her nose straighter, her

lips a bit thicker, and her skin a few tones lighter. All Tige seemed to have inherited from her was her skinniness.

He jumped down from the tub and walked back into the living room over to the window to look for the signs of Christmas day.

There were a couple of teenage boys streaking down the street on ten-speed bicycles. A tiny girl was zigzagging on a tricycle behind a group of children who were flashing new coats and shoes, a football, play guns, a wagon, a plastic riding toy, and four pair of skates among them. They seemed to be headed for the church parking lot two blocks away, which was the best playground in the area. Tige thought for a second of going there and asking to be included in their fun, but he decided against it. His mother had told him before not to bother, only he *had* bothered once or twice. Because he had nothing to trade or offer in playing, he was for the most part looked down upon. If one person refused him, others would take the same cue. If they did let him play with something of theirs, they were always afraid he'd break it or wouldn't want to give it back when he was told to.

Tige frowned. He'd be glad when Christmas was over and all those stupid toys banged up and broken. He left the window and headed for the kitchen. He had in mind some hot grits and sausage, but as he passed the table, something caught his eye that made him forget his original objective.

A brightly gift-wrapped package the size of a large shoe box lay on the table beside the tree. Tige stood gaping for a short while, not knowing exactly what to make of it. He examined the package closely without touching it. There was no card to say who it was intended for—but then who else could it be for, if not for him? He looked back at Marvin, who was still deep within his dreams, then he stared again at the present, feeling a strange surge of anticipation.

Tige lifted the present slowly, being careful of its five-pound weight, and walked over to the heater where he sat down on the floor, made himself comfortable, and eased the colored paper from the box. Inside the box lay a shiny new pair of skates.

A vivid smile etched itself across Tige's face. He took the skates and placed one against the bottom of his foot. It was way too large, and he frowned. But still, a gift was a gift, and it really was nice of Marvin to think so much of him. And besides, there were other ways to play with skates other than strapped to the feet. So Tige placed them side-by-side on the floor, and pretending that they were race cars, he zoomed them across the floor. He looked to see if the noise had awakened Marvin. It hadn't, so he continued with his kitchen-to-the-bathroom-with-a-detour-under-the-bed stock skate race.

After the race had been won, he lined them up and sat on them in order to row himself around the room. But after a time, he tired of this and ran and pounced upon the bed. He peeked over Marvin's shoulder, wondering how he could possibly have slept through all the noise.

"Hey Marv," he whispered in his ear. "Mar-r-r-rvin-n-n."

He sighed in dismay when there was no reaction, then took one of his skates and drove it from Marvin's foot up to his arm where a large hand reared up and captured it.

"Merry Christmas to you too," Marvin yawned.

Tige held up the skates. "Is these fo' me?" he asked hopefully.

"You'd feel mighty foolish right about now if they weren't, now wouldn't you? You like them?"

"Yea-a-ah. But..."

"What's wrong?"

"They too big."

"Too big? Can't be. Let me see."

Marvin examined the skates in comparison to Tige's foot, and immediately found the trouble.

"Oh, I see now. You don't have them adjusted. There should be a key somewhere. Go look in the box."

Tige dashed off the bed and returned with the box and its wrappings.

"I only wanted the key," Marvin grinned. He propped himself up on his pillow and took the key and one skate. "Let me have your right foot."

"Fo' how much?" questioned Tige, then he dumped his foot into Marvin's hand.

"Very funny. Now see, this is the way you get them to fit. Haven't you ever had a pair of skates before?"

"Nope."

Marvin fitted the skate on and slapped his hand across the bottom of the wheels.

"There you go. You can do the other one, can't you?"

"I thank so. You gonna come and teach me how ta skate?"

"Uh, not now. You go on out and try it by yourself awhile. I need some more sleep. I was up half the night trying to find a store still open to buy those things."

Marvin sank between the covers and turned on his side.

"Marvin-n-n," Tige pouted.

"Ti-i-ige—later. Much later."

Tige pulled in his pout and hopped around carefully on his left foot to get his coat, then hopped out the door.

Marvin slept for another ninety minutes then finally rose to start a pot of coffee brewing. He peeked out the window to see how Tige was getting along and found him clinging to a lamp post with his left skate dangling around his ankle by its strap. When he lifted his foot to try and swing the skate beneath, he fell unmercifully to the ground. Marvin grimaced as if he himself had felt the pain. It obviously wasn't very much fun for him out there alone, so Marvin slipped into his pants and two heavy sweaters to go to his aid.

Tige looked up as Marvin came bounding down the stairs with the broom in his hands.

"Having problems?" Marvin asked.

"I cain't git this stupid thang ta stay on."

"Here, let me do it for you."

"You come ta learn me how ta skate?"

"Yeah. I started to feel sorry for the sidewalk, the way you're banging on it."

"Very funny. What's the broom fo'?"

"For you."

Marvin held the broom out horizontally in front of Tige. "Grab hold of this and hang on tight," he said, then lifted Tige up, using his foot as a stopper to keep the skates from rolling. "You know how to walk? One step at a time, come on. Lean forward and keep your knees bent some— if you don't, you'll fall tail first."

He steered Tige up and down the streets, giving him more freedom from the broom as his confidence rose. Soon, Tige had mastered the art well enough to keep from falling and to coast free without assistance. Then he finally took a break for breakfast, which was by then lunch. Leaving his shoes in the skates, he pranced about the kitchen barefoot.

"I can see it now," Marvin said. "You'll be in either the roller derby or the winter Olympics as an ice skater, and I can watch and say that I bought him his first pair of skates."

"I didn't say thank you, did I?"

"Oh, you said it. Not in words... but you said it."

"You used the rent money on 'em?"

"Don't worry about it. We can make it up later."

"You sure?"

"I'm sure."

"Oh, I almost fa'got..."

Tige left the table to go rummage through his jacket. He came up with a small sack, from which he quickly tore a sales ticket off and balled it up in his hand. He came back to the table and presented the sack to Marvin.

"Didn't git a chance ta wrap it."

Marvin took the sack and acknowledged him with a timid smile. He opened it and pulled out two pairs of socks—one black and one brown—that were fortunately just his size and style. Tige looked on eagerly for approval.

Marvin gave him a delighted smile. "You must have been reading my mind... or going through my drawer. Thank you, Tige. I really appreciate it."

"You welcome.... Hey, you want me fo' anythang? I wanna go back outdo's."

"No, run along."

"Oh, is it all right if I go ta that parkin' lot up the street?"

"Of course. Just be careful. Have a good time."

Marvin went to the window and looked out with a smile on his face as Tige skated off down the street. He felt good about what he'd just done. It was worth ten bucks and more to see such happiness on Tige's face. And playing with him out there like that had been a delight also. It made Marvin feel a few years younger and a lot more alive than he'd felt in quite awhile. He was beginning to think how nice it would be if there could be more days like this one; he felt more fatherly toward Tige than he had his own children. He wished that he could provide better for Tige. A simple, shabby roof over his head, TV dinners, and a pair of skates were not enough. He wished that he could give him much more than that—a good home, clothes, an education, everything he was entitled to.

A crazy thought entered his mind. He wasn't so old that he couldn't make a comeback, especially since he had such a worthy cause. He'd read how many single persons were adopting children nowadays, and there were quite a few interracial adoptions also. Actually all he had to do was straighten himself out a bit. With his background and sheepskin it shouldn't be too hard to land a good-paying job. Knowing Tige, he'd probably say it was a stupid idea, then in the next breath turn right around and call him pappy. Marvin decided to keep his thoughts to himself until the right moment; no use in letting the cat out of the bag just yet. He had a lot more thinking to do to make sure this was what he wanted.

For now, he decided to blow some more of the rent money on a hot chicken dinner and a newspaper.

That evening, after reading Tige the comics, Marvin settled down with the newspaper to go over the classfied ads. After awhile Tige became nosy and came to look over his shoulder.

"What you lookin' at the want ads fo'? You lookin' ta see if anybody need a handyman?"

"Sort of."

"*Sort* of?"

"That's what I said."

"That's what you said, but what do you mean?"

"You have a nose problem, you know that?"

"If you ain't lookin' fo' no handyman job, I *know* ya cain't be lookin' fo' no *reg'lar* job."

"Oh, you do, do you? And why *can't* I be looking for a regular job?"

"*You?*" Tige snickered. "Man, you *gotta* be kiddin'."

"Hey, hey now, just wait a minute. What's so funny about me wanting a regular job? Come on, I'd like to know."

Seeing that Marvin was serious and becoming angry, Tige stopped laughing.

"Why'd you stop laughing? You thought it was funny, didn't you?"

"Nawl, I thought you was just jokin'."

"No, I'm not joking. I'm serious about this, okay?"

Tige nodded slowly. "Why?" he asked after a few seconds.

"Because I hear it's a good way to earn money."

"Thought you said you didn't need that much money ta live off anyway."

"No, *I* don't, but maybe you haven't noticed— there're two of us now."

"I can take care of myself."

"Sure you can. Steal your way right into jail. Besides, I'm not doing it just for you, I'm doing it for myself. I'm getting tired of living off TV dinners and canned food. I'm getting tired of this dump altogether. I'd like something different—better."

"Why all of a sudden? Yesterday you was in love with this dump."

"I have the right to change my mind, don't I?"

"You had *years* ta change yo' mind. What's so special about taday?"

"Tige, I don't have to sit here and answer your questions. I'm a grown man and I *don't* need your opinion, your permission, or anything else. If I want to work or rob a bank, that's my business and I don't have to answer to you. Do I make myself clear?"

Tige pouted at the tone of voice Marvin used, then nodded. He waited a moment before tapping Marvin lightly on the arm.

"What?" Marvin asked trying to hold down his temper.

"You gonna 'pologize now or later?" Tige asked calmly.

"Apologize for what?"

"You always 'pologize when you holla at me like that."

"Oh, for crying out...All right, all right, you win. Let's start over. I have been doing some thinking and I feel like there's something missing from my life. I just sort of miss some of the finer things in life. I'm used to better things and I didn't mind living without them before, but, uh, I'm not getting any younger, and I have to think about my future. Five years from now I probably won't be able to climb houses and haul junk and do all the things I can now. The old arteries are going to start tightening up soon. I don't have any kind of pension, nothing to fall back on. I'd be just another old man on welfare. So while I've still got time, I'd like to do something about it. Is that okay with you?"

"What kinda job you gonna git?"

"A nice sit-down, easy one, hopefully in advertising. That's what I was doing before."

"I thought you didn't like what you was befo'e. You said you hated it—that's why you left."

"I didn't hate the *job*, just didn't care that much for some of the people."

"Well how you know dese new people gonna be any dif'rent?"

"I can handle it. I know I can. Don't you want me to

work? There's a lot of things I could do with the money. Wouldn't you like a television set? Color?"

Tige shrugged his shoulders. "That's up ta you if you wanna git one."

"Up to *me*? I don't understand. Are you against my bringing home some extra money?"

"You can brang as much as you want, but *I* won't be heah."

"Now what's that supposed to mean? You planning on running away?"

"Well what you 'spect me ta do everyday while you off at work, sit heah and twiddle my thumbs?"

"Oh . . . I see."

"Yeah, the way it is now, we both go ta work. But *yo'* way, you go ta work and I stay heah all day long sit'in' around with nothin' ta do."

"Nothing to do. Nothing to do, did you say? Obviously you haven't taken a very good look around this apartment lately. Just look at it. The windows need washing, the walls need painting, the floors need mopping, the kitchen cabinets need cleaning out, the bathroom needs . . ."

"Hey, hey, hey, wait a minute. I ain't no housewife now."

"I thought you wanted something to do."

"If I wanted to be a *slave*, I'd go back to the cotton fields. What you thank I am? You must be crazy, man."

"No, you were just complaining that if I went off to work, you'd die of boredom. I was just trying to think of some things to brighten your life."

"You *still* crazy."

"That's just the way I see things. If I go out everyday to bring in some money, the least you could do is help straighten up around here. Never knew you were so lazy. Glad I found it out."

"I ain't *lazy*. I could clean this old raggedy hole up fifty times befo'e you even walked out the do'."

"*Sure* you could," Marvin grunted.

"I *could*. You 'on't believe me?"

"Before I walked out the door?"

"Well, not *that* fast. But I bet ya befo'e you came home."

"Tige."

"What?"

"Go to bed."

"See, if you were gone all mornin' or somethin', I could..."

"*Good night*, Tige."

"Night."

"You late," said Tige when Marvin opened his eyes.

"Late for what?"

"Just late. You been sleepin' just 'bout all day. It's after twelve a'clock."

"So. Didn't have anything special to do anyway."

"It's Sadday. You gotta go ta the wash house and the groc'ry sto'e, or is we gonna eat this week?"

"What if I told you I didn't have any money for groceries?"

"Not even a nickel?"

"Not even a penny."

"Well, you ain't got none, you just ain't got none. We still got somethin' in the cabinets. We ain't ready ta starve yet."

"Would you be willing to sit up here and starve with me if I really didn't have anything?"

"Nawl, I ain't *that* crazy. I'd go out and find me somethin'."

"Don't worry, you won't have to. I lied. I *do* have some money. Just feeling a little lazy, that's all."

Tige put his hand on Marvin's forehead to check for a
fever.

"No, I'm not sick."

"Somethin's wrong with you. You got gas?"

"No."

"Constipated?"

"No."

"You cain't be pregnant."

"Tige, how would you like one across your mouth?"

"Yeah, you and what army?"

Marvin turned on him menacingly but Tige backed
away quickly.

"Don't you hit me man, I'll call the NAACP on you."

Marvin broke into hearty laughter and clapped his
hands together.

"I'll be going to the store in half an hour. Go skate."

"Okay."

While Tige spent the day out skating, Marvin decided
that a good first step toward getting himself straightened
out would be to do something he should have done a long
time ago—call Miss Carrie and let her know that Tige was
all right. The poor woman was probably worried sick
about him.

He found a telephone booth and leafed through the
white pages only to find himself out of luck. There was no
listing for a Carrie Carter. He wondered if he was
remembering it correctly, then considered the possibility
that perhaps she didn't own a phone.

"Boulevard," he recalled. "Nine-something-some-
thing Boulevard. Oh well, I guess I'd better."

He slapped the book closed and made his way for
Boulevard, getting lost twice after asking directions from
people who were guessing his destination. He finally
came to a vicinity that lead him to believe he was on the

right track. A wide variety of men lined a section of the opposite street in front of a barbecue shack. The men ranged in age from twenty to sixty or more. Most were ragged bums with bare mouths and drunken eyes, sockless and nearly shoeless. They lounged around the front of the little shack, smoking, drinking, and telling stories loaded with profanity. They glanced at Marvin indifferently. Seeing that he was the wrong color in the wrong neighborhood didn't bother them. It wasn't any of their business what he was doing there, and even if it were they weren't the type to do anything about it.

Marvin looked about at the cluttered and broken sidewalks and the buildings that were crumbling but still occupied. It was easy to see why Tige had such low regard for his future. The place was horribly dismal; it was shameful that it even existed. But it did, because the people in the area had nothing better. Some would make it out, but there were others that probably felt the same as Tige.

As Marvin neared an intersection, he could just make out the street sign Boulevard Pl. He was about to pass the second to the last building on the block when a woman's slender leg, clad in sheer black hose, popped out in front of him. He peered around the corner of the stairway to see what was connected to it.

A less than attractive young woman dressed in a black miniskirt, a deeply low-cut blouse, and a long, flowing red wig smiled down at him from atop the third step. She jerked her head toward the door at the top of the stairs. Marvin smiled, embarrassed, then caught sight of another figure coming up from behind him. She was a little bit better looking and wore a skin-tight pantsuit with buttons that looked as if they were about to pop open.

Marvin backed away from them both and shrugged

his shoulders. "Not unless you're willing to take small change," he said. "Very small change."

The women grunted and turned away.

"Sorry ladies. Maybe next time."

"My mama's bread-d-d-d-d is burnin' and it cain't git out!" came a loud chant of children's voices from around the corner. Marvin turned the corner and approached a group of little people as they held hands in a circle and repeated the chant over and over.

"Mama's bread," as Marvin came to understand it, was the little girl inside the circle. The circle itself was an oven. The bread had to break out of the oven to keep from burning. The bread and oven all giggled and screamed deliriously until finally one of the many oven doors was broken open and the bread escaped safely. Marvin grinned, amused at the game, then detoured around them.

He walked along Boulevard, eyeing the numbers on the buildings carefully until he found one that seemed vaguely familiar. He read the names off the mailboxes in the hallway, but none were Miss Carrie's. He tried two other buildings and then came to one where a teenage boy sat atop the concrete bannister, quietly puffing on a cigarette.

Marvin would have liked to ignore him, but unfortunately the feeling wasn't mutual. When he got to the third step, the jagged end of a broken off broomstick touched the center of his chest. The young man at the opposite end looked down his keen, wide nose and spoke to him.

"What you want 'round heah, whitey?" Mojoe said with an air of authority.

"I beg your pardon?"

"I know everybody who comes and goes 'round heah and you ain't one of 'em. So what you doin' heah?"

"Oh, I see.... But, uh, what gives you the idea that what I'm doing here is any of your business?" Marvin asked, also with an air of authority.

Mojoe blew out a ring of smoke and smiled slyly.

"What gives you the idea it *ain't?*"

Marvin saw that getting past Mojoe would be a small hassle, and decided there would probably be no harm in confiding in him.

"Okay, then maybe you *can* help me. I'm looking for Mrs. Carrie Carter. You know her?"

"That all depends. What you want her fo'? You a cop?"

"No, it's nothing like that. I just wanted to talk to her."

"'Bout what?"

"It's about a little fellow who used to live around here somewhere. His name is Tige Jackson."

"Oh, *Tige*. What ever happened to that li'l' jerk? They was gonna stick him in a orphanage or someplace. Li'l' joker took off and nobody seen him since."

"Except me," Marvin confessed. "He's been staying with me all this time and he happened to mention Mrs. Carter to me and I thought I'd just come and let her know he was all right."

"Oh. So what is you, one of them Big Brothers or somethin'?"

"Yes, something like that. By the way, you didn't say—*does* Mrs. Carter stay here?"

"Yeah. Second flo', 'partment 2B."

"Thank you. Do you mind?" Marvin asked and pointed to the stick still at his chest. Mojoe removed the stick and allowed him to pass.

Marvin went upstairs in search of apartment 2B. He found it easily and rapped gently on the door.

"Who is it?" came a young girl's voice from beyond the door.

"My name is Marvin Stewart. I'd like to talk to Mrs. Carter about Tige Jackson."

"Mama," said the voice as it moved away from the door. "Somebody wanna talk to you about Tiger."

Within a few seconds, the door opened slightly and a woman peered at him past the chain of a safety latch.

"You with the Welfare people?"

"No, ma'am. I'm a friend of Tige's. I've been taking care of him."

"Is he all right? I didn't know *what* had happened to the po' child after his mama died."

"He's doing fine. That's what I came to tell you."

"Oh, wait just a second."

The door closed as she unfastened the chain.

"Come on in and have a seat."

"Thank you."

He followed her into the living room and sat opposite her on the sofa.

"I been so worried about him. I was 'spectin' ta heah about him being found dead somewhere, but *you* been takin' care of him?"

"Yes, I ran into him one night and haven't been able to get rid of him. Not that I've really tried. He's not that fond of the Welfare authorities."

"Yeah, well, Vanessa had a lot of trouble with them. So I guess he got that from her. They were gonna come fo' him. I guess that's why he ran away. They probably wouldn't have kept him long anyway."

"How's that?"

"Well, just give 'em a li'l' time, they would've tracked down that no good daddy of his. See, what it was, Vanessa wanted to marry Richard ever since she met him and she figured if she had his baby, she could hold on ta him. Didn't work though, 'cause Richard knew what he wanted and *she* wa'n't in his plans. He stuck around awhile ta help pay bills, but then they had a big fight. That's when we both moved heah. *I* moved 'cause I needed a bigger place, and *she* moved ta try and f'a'git *him*. That's been, oh, eight—nine years ago. He's still in Atlan'a though. I've seen him a coupla times ridin' 'round in his Cadillac. And he don't care two cents 'bout that child. But I bet if the authorities had gotten on his case, he would've got off his tail and did somethin' then."

"Is somethin' wrong?" Carrie asked when she saw that Marvin was lost in thought.

"Mmm? No, no. Just thinking about something."

"Well, listen, I don't know how much good it'd do, but I got an old phone number fo' Richard if you wanna try and git in touch with him. Maybe he's changed over the years. He may be willin' to take Tige off your hands. You want it?"

"Mmm? Oh, yes, thank you."

"Shirley," she called out toward one of the bedrooms.

"Mam?"

"Look in that top drawer of the dresser and brang me that gold address book."

She turned back to Marvin. "Vanessa didn't have no phone, so she always used mine. I have a number fo' Richard, but I thank it was probably at his job because she could only use it durin' the day befo'e five."

Marvin nodded in agreement and looked up as Shirley walked into the room carrying her mother's address book. She had her mother's features and the look of a thirteen-year-old. What was surprising to Marvin was her figure. Through the roomy smock she wore, Marvin could well distinguish a pair of oversized breasts and a belly that gave the impression that she swallowed a small watermelon whole. Marvin stared at her as she came nearer. She gave the book to Carrie and stood at her side for a moment.

"Y'all find Tiger?" she asked Marvin as if he were more than one person.

"Yeah," answered her mother. "This man's takin' care of him."

"Oh. Is he comin' back heah?"

"No, I don't think so," Marvin told her. "I believe there're a few too many memories here for him."

"Oh. Well, tell him I said hey."

"I will," Marvin assured her, then he watched her turn and disappear the way she came.

"It's a shame, ain't it?" Carrie said.

"Pardon?"

"What's the business a baby got havin' a baby? Chillun these days—learn thangs too quick or either too late. Try and tell 'em one thang, they do another; goes in one ear and out the other."

Carrie leafed through the book a few seconds, then came to a halt.

"Heah it is," she said, handing it to Marvin. "All I got is the number. I guess you can find out somethin' from it. Just tear it out, I 'on't thank I'll ever need it ag'in. . . . What you gonna do if you 'on't find him?"

Marvin smiled a half smile. "I don't know," he said. "I'm not sure of what I'll do if I *should* find him. He probably wouldn't want him."

"But then ag'in he might. Never can tell what people'll do sometimes. Take you—tryin' ta help someone ain't even yo' own color. You must be a mighty kind man."

"Thank you. And thank you for your help."

He rose to leave, and she escorted him to the door.

"I hope you have some luck at whatever you do 'bout Tige. He deserves somethin' good fo' a change."

"I'll let you know what happens. Goodbye."

Tige's father, of all things, Marvin thought. At first he was afraid that his plans for adopting Tige were ruined.

But on second thought, Marvin decided that since Tige's father had deserted him, he probably didn't want to be bothered with the boy; he probably could care less whether his son was alive or dead. Besides, he had never married Vanessa, so he actually had no real legal claim to Tige. Marvin's plans were still intact, though he'd try extra hard to hurry them along. As for Richard, Marvin dismissed him from his mind.

Marvin paced back and forth in front of the bathroom door waiting for Tige to come out.

"Tige, hurry up. What are you doing in there?"

"What *do* folks do in bathrooms?" Tige answered. "What you wanna do in heah?"

"What do people generally do in bathrooms?" said Marvin.

"I *know* what *people* do—I wanna know what *you* gonna do. Heh. Heh."

"Very funny. You're cracked."

Marvin waited impatiently and minutes later the toilet was flushed and Tige appeared outside the bathroom, shaking his wet hands dry.

"'Bout time. You know that's what towels are for," Marvin told him as he started past him on his way in, only to be confronted with an appalling and very recognizable odor. He scowled and fanned the air in front of his nose. Tige eyed him and grunted.

"I'd like ta see *you* leave it smellin' like a rose."

"Anything would be an improvement."

Marvin flapped his hand and walked past the scented barrier to the cabinet above the sink.

"Hey, Marv, you gonna shave?"

"Among other things."

"Can I watch? I mean shave, not the among other thangs."

"Just don't get in my way. Shaving takes concentration."

"I ain't gonna bother ya," Tige promised. He sat down on the edge of the bathtub, but seeing that his view was obstructed by Marvin's back, he climbed on top of the toilet seat on Marvin's left. He bent one knee on the tank top which just about brought him to Marvin's height.

He looked at Marvin's reflection in the mirror as it began to apply shaving cream to one side of the face.

"Let me do this side," Tige pleaded.

Marvin glanced at him through the mirror.

"Thought you weren't going to bother me."

"I just wanna help," Tige spoke in an angelic voice.

Marvin could see the disappointment starting up in his face, so he handed him the can of shaving cream.

"Here. Just push that button there."

Tige took it in hand and proceeded to spread the cream lavishly onto Marvin's face.

"Hey, that's enough."

"Nawl, wait a sec . . . right dare. Dare, that's good."

Tige recapped the can and wiped his hand on the towel around Marvin's neck, then watched as Marvin picked up his razor. He let the blade float gently down three inches of his cheek, erasing lather and tiny brown hairs.

"How old do ya have ta be ta shave?" Tige asked him.

"It doesn't always depend on your age. Some boys start getting hairy at fifteen—some a little earlier and some a lot later. Some never get a chance to shave. Depends on whether hairiness runs in the family."

"How old was you when you started shavin'?"

"I was a slow starter. Didn't really get into it until I was somewhere in my twenties. Even now, I don't get that much. I can go a week or two without getting stubble. Some men have to shave twice a day."

Marvin finished with his right side and started for the left.

"Let me do this side," Tige pleaded again.

"Only if you want to see me bleed."

"Come on, Marvin," Tige pouted disappointedly. "Let me just do it one time."

"Tige, I am not going to give up my skin for your enjoyment. You know razors have blades in them. Blades are very sharp objects and my face is very subject to feeling pain."

"I'll be careful. Come on, man-n-n-n."

Marvin sighed and gave in to him.

"I'm spoiling you, you know that. Need to have my head examined. Here."

He gave the razor to Tige.

"Okay, what do I do? Just..."

"Just be careful. Hold it like that and move slowly and gently."

Marvin watched him in the mirror and held his breath as Tige cut a clear path through the foam and came to a halt at the bottom of his cheek."

"Gawd!" was Tige's only comment after this astonishing feat. Marvin exhaled deeply and took the razor from him.

"I second the emotion."

"See, man, I told ya I wa'n't gonna hurt cha. I knowed what I was doin'."

"Is that so? Why is it, I saw my life flashing before my eyes just then?"

"Bull. You know I did good."

"Yeah, but you don't mind if I take over from here; I don't think my heart can stand another good job like that."

Marvin continued to scrape away the lather while Tige watched him gravely with a hand on his shoulder.

"You git'in' gray, Marv."

"Better than going bald."

"Oh. You mean if you turn gray, you ain't gonna go baldheaded?"

"It works that way at times. If you lose your hair first, there really isn't any reason to turn gray now, is there?"

"Nope, guess not. How old is you, Marv?"

"I'm fifty-three, Tige."

"Fo' real? You 'on't look that old."

"Thank you."

"'Cause I thought when you got around fifty, you turn all gray and dried up. You ain't even dried up."

"Thank you again."

"How tall is you?"

"I see you're full of questions again. I'm six-feet-three."

"It'd take two of me ta make one of you, wouldn't it? How you git so tall?"

"I grew that way, Tige."

"Oh. Well, why you grow *that* tall?"

"I didn't—I mean—no one has control over how tall they grow. When your body is ready to, it stops on its own. And I thought you said you weren't going to bother me."

"I won't no mo'e," Tige promised—and kept the promise for only a moment.

"What's them black dots in the middle of yo' eyes?"

"They're called pupils. You have them, too. Your eyes

are so dark, you probably never paid much attention to
them."

Tige swung his face point blank to the mirror.

"Oh yeah, I see 'em now. But you can see yo's bedder
'cause yo' eyes blue. How yo' eyes git that color?"

"Hereditary. My eyes are blue because my parents'
eyes were blue. It's a genetic trait that runs in my family."

"Well how come yo' fam'ly eyes is blue and mine is
black?"

"I don't quite get the question, Tige."

"I'm sayin' is, how come I cain't have blue eyes too?"

"You don't have blue eyes because you're black. The
black race wasn't intended to have blue eyes or light skin
or blonde hair. And the only reason some do is because of
the mixing of the races. You understand now?"

"Yeah, but how come black people is so dark and
white people is so light?"

Tige grabbed Marvin's hand and held it next to his
own.

"See dare. That's what I'm talkin' 'bout."

"Well, skin coloring has to do with pigment. There's
this substance called pigment in the blood, and it
determines your color. If you have a lot—and most blacks
do—then you come out dark. And if you barely have any,
you come out light."

"But..."

"But what?" Marvin sighed, weary from the question-
ing.

"But how come it's just blacks who got a lotta
pigmy..."

"Pigment."

"Pigment, and come out dark? And why do whites
come out light? And another thang, it ain't just color. How
come blacks have nappy hair and rounded off noses and

big lips, and whites git ta have straight pretty hair, and why is *Japanese* people yellowly with slanted eyes, and Indians have big noses and black, black hair, and . . ."

"In other words," Marvin stopped him, "why are people black, white, red, and yellow. You're asking why are people different. Well, it'd be a pretty dull-looking world if everyone looked the same, now wouldn't it?"

"Yeah, but the way it is now, it's just causin' a lotta trouble. People hate each other 'cause they different. That don't make no sense."

"I know it doesn't, I know it doesn't."

Marvin splashed his face with water, dried himself, and turned his full attention to Tige.

"Let me ask you something. Do you believe in God?"

"My mama said he's fo' real."

"And you believe your mother?"

"Yeah."

"All right then, if you believe in God, then you should believe that it was his idea to make people different. He's the one whose responsible for people being black and white and every other color there is, and for giving us the physical features we all have. It's his world, and he did things the way he wanted to. You believe that?"

"Yeah, but he 'pose ta see everythang and know everythang—don't he know how much trouble he causin' that way? Everybody hatin' everybody and killin' and wars goin' on. I thought he was 'pose ta be all good. How come he let all that stuff happen?"

"Because . . . I don't know—I guess because he's just waiting for us to learn things for ourselves. He gave us a brain to think with, and the ability to love and understand, and maybe he's just waiting for us to put them to use."

"But, man," Tige frowned, "that stuff's been goin' on

fa years and years. Ain't he *ever* gonna come help us?"

"Tige, calm down. I know what you're thinking. It *is* a pretty gloomy world once you stop to think about it, but if you look back a little, you'll see we've come a long way. Start with this country here, the U.S. Where else could you find a bigger variety of people living peacefully in one area? There are no wars here. People have their disagreements, yes, but bit by bit we're working things out. Slavery—it's gone. No one can spit on you and keep you from going to school these days. See, that's something at least. People are finally beginning to treat each other like people and not like colors. It's getting where people don't even see colors anymore. Like when I first saw you—all I could see was a black child. But now, I see more than that. I see Tige Jackson—you. Tell me what you see when you look at me."

Tige studied Marvin's face a moment, then spoke.

"You used ta be just a white man. Seem like you the same as me now—not black, but the same some kinda way."

"See, that's God's plan, I think. It's taken thousands of years to come this far, and it'll probably take a thousand more, but maybe he figures, yes, we'll make mistakes, and we'll learn from them. And someday we might make his world the way he would have liked it."

Tige curled up the right side of his mouth with nothing more to add to the subject.

Marvin turned back to the mirror to slap on some aftershave lotion. "You know," he said between slaps, "for someone who doesn't even know what a question mark is, you ask some pretty good ones."

"Fo' somebody who keeps sayin' I 'on't know—you do."

"Well, the lessons are over for now. How 'bout taking a walk while I finish up here."

"Okay." Tige jumped to the floor and exited. "Don't fall in the toilet."

Marvin appeared a half hour later, his hair neatly combed and his body smelling of soap.

"Hey, you know what?" said Marvin as he dressed.

"What?"

"I feel good. I really feel wondrously, stupendously good. And you know what else?"

"What?"

"I'm going to do something I have absolutely no business doing."

"Like what?"

"Celebrate."

"Celebrate what? Is taday your birthday?"

"No, something even better. This is my very own special Independence Day. I have some money in the bank and since we're all caught up with our bills, what say we go celebrate."

"Yea-a-a-a! What we gonna do?"

"Let's see, what can we do?" Marvin mused, then he looked Tige up and down. "What size clothes do you wear?"

"Big economy size. How should *I* know? Never had nothin' ta fit yet. Why?"

"You'll see. Come on."

Marvin headed for the bank with Tige as his shadow and withdrew the last of his funds in reserve. Once the account had contained nearly three-hundred dollars, but he had been making constant withdrawals in Tige's behalf. Since Tige had come to live with him, his food bills had tripled because of Tige's voracious appetite, and gas and light bills had increased because Tige's companionship kept him home more. But he had to admit it was all money well spent.

"Are you ready to celebrate?"

"Yeah. What we gonna do?"

"First off, we're going to buy you some clothes, then we will feast, make merry, and all out splurge, my boy, splurge."

"Hey, I 'on't drank."

Marvin grinned and shook his head. "Son, you have got a *lot* to learn. Come on."

Tige's clothes before had always been hand-me-downs and handouts from neighbors or pickups from the Salvation Army store, which were sometimes pretty good but always oversized to allow for growth. He rarely outgrew them, just outwore them. Now he was being fitted with a suit—his very first. It was brown with white stitching along the seams and pockets. The pants and jacket followed the contour of his slim body and hung just so all the way around.

The purchase of the suit was followed up with shoes, socks, a shirt and tie set, and underclothes. The outfit itself was complete, but the work wasn't quite finished yet.

Marvin studied Tige's hair. Long lumps of tight, reddish brown curls covered his head and seemed to dare the entrance of a comb. Something had to be done for it.

"Hey, Marv, you gonna git yo'self somethin'?"

"No. I have plenty stuffed away in mothballs. Let's just concentrate on you."

"Well where we **goin'** now?"

"Right here."

Marvin shifted the packages he held to one hand and pointed Tige through the glass doors of a barbershop. Fortunately, a barber stood beside an unoccupied chair. He looked down at Tige and smiled.

"I *know* I don't have to ask if I can help *you*," he said comicly.

Marvin set all the packages on a chair and pushed Tige gently toward the black man, whose nameplate read Cullen.

"I want to see if you can't shear some of that wool off him, will you?"

"Hey, man," Tige objected, "I ain't no sheep."

"When you cut it," Marvin continued, "put it in a bag for me—might take it and knit me a sweater."

"I ain't gonna git *all* my hair cut off now."

"Don't worry. The man's a barber—he knows how much to take off and how much to leave. Although, if he did give you a crewcut, you wouldn't need another haircut for three years."

"Ha, ha," Tige sounded off sarcastically, then climbed into the chair.

"How long do you think that's going to take?" Marvin asked Cullen.

"That all depends. When's the last time this stuff's been washed?"

"It ain't *stuff*—it's *hair*," Tige corrected him sourly.

"Shut up. It might be able to pass for hair when he gets through with it. I guess you'd better give him a shampoo and do whatever you can for him," Marvin told Cullen.

"Well," smiled Cullen, "I always did like a challenge."

"Marv, you gonna wait fo' me?"

"I believe I may even join you. I think I'm about due for a slight trim."

Marvin took a seat and waited his turn for the second chair. He noted that Tige was having quite a time of it. The shampoo revealed an even greater length of hair, and he seemed to grimace at every phase of the ordeal. After drying, he was faced with the greater problem of having it combed out.

Marvin's turn came soon, and he indulged himself in a quick trim. He occasionally glanced over and saw gobs of hair dropping onto the floor and onto Tige's shoulders, with little visible difference on his head. Tige squeezed his eyes shut only to keep the hair out, but looked as if he was in great agony.

"It doesn't hurt that bad, does it?" Marvin asked him.

"Don't you say a word ta me . . ." Tige began, but had to stop to spit out some hair.

Marvin grinned and spoke to Cullen. "Be careful of that. I once saw an eagle fly out of there."

Tige frowned, but not wanting another mouthful of hair, he ignored him.

After his own haircut, Marvin took an admiring look in the mirror. He appreciated the clean, even sideburns and the way the front of his hair swept over to the left and clung neatly in place. He had to admit to himself, that even with thirty or forty gray strands, he looked at least three years younger.

He picked up a magazine and sat down to wait for Tige, who thirty minutes later finally began to look transformed. The true color of his hair was revealed as a deep chocolate brown dotted with white speckles of reflected light. He was now the proud owner of a smooth round globe—soft and lustrous.

Excess hair was wiped away from his face and neck and his bib was removed. He was swiveled around to face the mirrors and was very surprised at what he saw. It was a whole different him—like comparing a clipped poodle to a sheepdog.

"Damn," he whispered under his breath, then turned around to Marvin. "Hey, dig this, Marvin. I'm cute."

"By George, I believe you are. And who says miracles don't happen?"

They left the barbershop and their discarded hair behind and returned home, where Marvin urged Tige to take a quick bath.

"What I gotta take a bath fo'? We goin' somewhere?"

"We're going out to dinner. You're going to wear your new suit."

"Just ta go eat?"

"We are not going to just eat, we are going to *dine*. There's a big difference. I'm tired of having nothing but canned goods and hamburgers. I'm ready for some *real* food. Lobster, shrimp, steak—*real* food. Now get in that tub so we can get ready. And don't take all day. You can go scuba diving some other time. And use some of my deodorant under your arms. Your puberty is becoming telltale."

"What?"

"I said, you're beginning to stink."

Tige lifted his arm and sniffed, then frowned at the odor.

"I thank I see what cha mean."

He turned on his heels and headed for the bathroom. Marvin used the time while Tige was bathing to lay out both their clothes. After his bath, Tige waited patiently in his new underwear and socks for Marvin to take his turn in the tub.

"You could've put your clothes on," Marvin told him when he appeared from the bathroom. "You didn't have to wait for me."

"You git funny about thangs sometimes. I didn't wanna take no chances."

"Go ahead and get dressed."

Tige dressed in the same order that Marvin did. When it came to putting on his tie, he let Marvin take care of that. As a return favor, he had to handle Marvin's cufflinks.

"Now, let's see what we look like," said Marvin once they were fully dressed. He opened the closet door to expose the full length mirror attached to it, then stood with Tige in front of it. "Well, what do you think?"

"Gawd!" Tige smiled enthusiastically over the similarity of their suits and overall appearance. "We look just alike, don't we?"

"I believe we do at that."

"Where we goin' ta eat?"

"Oh, I'm not sure yet. Been so long since I've been to a restaurant, I don't know which one would be best for us. But there're plenty downtown. Just try and find one that's close to the bus stop. Okay, I guess we're ready to go now. Get your coat."

Tige took his army jacket from the doorknob of the closet and began to put it on.

"Ti-i-ige!" Marvin grimaced.

"What?"

"Why didn't you remind me to get you a new coat?"

"Why didn't you *tell* me ta remind you? You was the one doin' all the buyin'. How was I 'pose ta know what all you wanted?"

"You *knew* you needed a coat—why didn't you say something? Just look at you. Can't go around looking like that."

"I *been* goin' 'round lookin' like this."

"I know but..." Marvin looked at his watch and studied the time. "Stores'll be closed by the time we get there. It's too cool for you not to wear anything. Well, let me see if I can't find something a little better than that."

He went through his closet and pulled out an old leather jacket of his which was still in fairly good condition.

"This'll be big on you, but at least it looks better than that green thing you've got."

He handed it to Tige and helped him on with it. For someone Marvin's height and build, it would have been a perfect fit, but poor Tige was lost in it. He even had trouble locating his hands through the ends of the sleeves. Marvin looked at him and sighed.

"Why do you have to be so small?"

"I'm just right,"Tige told him. "It's yo' *coat* that's the wrong size."

"Well it's a cinch you can't wear that. Probably break your neck just trying to walk in it." He took the jacket away and rehung it. "And that was the best I could do."

"I'll just have ta wear my own coat then, 'less you wanna stay heah and go some other time. Open up a can of soup and fix a baloney samich."

"No way. Put that thing on and let's get out of here. I'm starving."

Marvin picked a quaint restaurant in Underground Atlanta. A southern belle of a hostess welcomed them at the entrance and led them with a big wide smile to their table. Then she excused herself to go back to her station.

"Tige, just lay your coat on this extra chair here."

Tige followed Marvin's example and folded his jacket neatly in place on the chair, then sat down and pulled his chair up to the table.

"What do you think so far?" Marvin asked.

"Whatever they cookin' sho do smell good."

A young man dressed in a bright red vest and a straw hat brought them both a glass of water and a menu.

"Hi, I'm George. I'll be back in a few minutes to take your orders."

Tige looked at his menu peculiarly. "What's this?" he asked Marvin.

"That's a menu."

"Oh. Do I eat it now or later?"

"I keep forgetting I have to speak simple English to you. You do not eat a menu. You eat what's on it."

"You mean all these heah words and thangs come off?"

"No, silly, of course not. Stop that. A menu is a list of foods that the restaurant is serving, as if you didn't know. Now, what would you like to eat?"

"They got any chicken?"

"Sure. Which would you like, chicken fricassee, chicken cacciatore, chicken a la king..."

"How 'bout chicken *fried*?"

"Fried chicken, Tige. You can get that anytime. Why not try something new and different."

"Well what you gonna have?"

"I've already got my mind made up about that. I'm going to have a great big giant lobster."

"Lobster? What's that?"

"You mean you don't even know what a lobster is? Child, where have you been all your life? A lobster is a sea creature—it's, uh, well you've seen crabs before, haven't you? On cartoons or what have you. You know those little things that come up on the beach and have shells and claws?"

The way Marvin snapped his fingers to demonstrate the claws of crabs, Tige visualized seeing the animal once or twice.

"Yeah, I know what you talkin' 'bout now. But what's a lobster?"

"A lobster is related to a crab. It's about this long, sometimes bigger, red, and it has these snapping claws similar to a crab. And they fish them out of the ocean for people to eat. Think you'd like one? They're really good."

"Yeah, you thought that darn straw was good too, didn't cha?"

"Okay, I'll tell you what. I'll order one for myself and let you have a taste and you can go ahead and order something of your own. What would you like?"

"They got any T-bone steak?"

"Sure. Have you ever had one before?"

"Nawl, but at least I know what it looks like."

"Nearly everyone likes steak, so you should get along with that a lot better. What would you like with that? Baked potato sound all right?"

"Yeah."

"Green salad?"

"Yeah. And some yella co'n and some light bread and a choc'lit milkshake."

"A complete rainbow. He's coming back to take our orders now."

"Hey, George," said Tige.

"Hi there," George replied bright and courteously. "Can I take you gentlemen's orders now?"

"Yes, I'd like the lobster plate special."

"Yes sir. Would you like wine to go with that?"

Marvin noticed the look he was getting from Tige so he declined the suggestion.

"No, some iced tea will be fine."

George wrote it down and turned to Tige. "All right, and what can I get for you?"

"I wanna T-bone steak and a baked potato and some yella co'n and two slices of light bread, and uh, what I leave out?" he asked Marvin.

"The salad and the milkshake."

"Oh yeah. And I wanna green salad and a choc'lit milkshake."

"I'm sorry but we don't serve milkshakes. How about just some chocolate milk?"

"Put some ice in it."

"Okey dokey. Be back shortly."

"He kinda nice," Tige commented on George after he'd left.

"That's his job to be nice. If he comes around with a rotten attitude and does a rotten job at serving people, he knows he won't get a very good tip."

"Why you have ta tip 'em fo' anyway? I see it on television sometimes. The guy gotta tip the waiter ten bucks just ta git a table. That don't even sound right."

"Well that's just the way it is. I don't know how on earth it got started, but they only get paid a certain amount of money and for the rest of their income they depend upon the generosity of the customers."

"So he just bein' nice and smiley ta budder you up so you'll give him a big tip?"

"Not necessarily. He may be that way all the time even when he's not looking for a tip. You know, this is a really nice place. Have you ever come down here before?"

"Yeah, every year."

"You mean you have a special time to come down?"

"Yeah. They have these festivals down heah every year. They have bands and innertainment, and arts and crafts, and all this homemade food layin' out on big tables."

"Ah! Food, the magic word. Knew there had to be something in it for you."

"Hey, I don't come just fo' the food. I listen to the

music and watch the innertainment, and look at the arts and crafts, *then* I go after the food."

"Were they giving out free samples?"

"Yeah, I got free samples—everytime they wa'n't lookin'. Them li'l', fat, country white ladies sho can cook. I wish that kid would hurry up with the food. I'm hungry."

Marvin reached for a bowl on the table and handed Tige one pack of the small crackers. "Here, nibble on these for awhile."

"Is these free?"

"*Are* they free."

"*Are* they free?"

"Yes. But that doesn't mean for you to take the whole bowl."

"Why not—if they free?"

"You have to be considerate and leave some for other people."

"What if *they* take 'em all?"

"Then you can point to them and say how inconsiderate and greedy they are."

"Aw, Marv, you ain't no fun at all."

"There's not a blessed thing wrong with you acting like a gentleman for a change. Who knows, you may even get to like it and grow up to be just like George."

"You mean actin' like a gentleman make you grow up ta be white?"

Marvin shook his head pitifully and opened a pack of crackers for himself. "You're hopeless. Absolutely hopeless."

When the food came, Tige was joyfully enthusiastic over his first steak, but when he saw what Marvin was having, his stomach turned slightly.

"What the heck is that thang?"

"Lobster," Marvin smiled. "Remember the creature I was telling you about?"

"You gonna eat that?"

"Of course, that's why I ordered it. It's very good."

"Looks like it's still alive."

"It *was* alive quite a few minutes ago, but it's a little more than dead now."

"They just now killed it fo' ya?"

"Yes, that's the way you have to do them. You have to keep them alive until you're ready to cook them. Then you just dump them into a pot and boil them, and after they're done, you put them on plates and you dig in like this. . . ."

Tige watched with a weak stomach as Marvin cut into the lobster and hoisted a piece of meat to his mouth. "Mmmm! That is delicious. Hey, come on, have a little piece and see if you like it."

Tige shrank away from the tidbit Marvin was holding out on the tip of his fork.

"Come on. Try it. Just a little."

Tige hesitated a while then finally took it. The taste of it actually wasn't so bad, but as Tige stared at the thing on the plate and thought of it's being alive and crawling around only minutes before, he felt his stomach about to heave. He moved the food to one side of his mouth so he could talk.

"Where do I spit this out at?"

"You *don't* spit it out, you *swallow* it."

"Well where do I *throw it up* after I swallow it?"

"Use your napkin. And keep your head low so you don't spoil anyone's appetite—especially mine."

Tige spat into the napkin and folded it up securely.

"Hey, George, come heah a minute."

George was cleaning off a table next to them when Tige called, but he stopped what he was doing to come to him.

"Yeah, what can I do for you?"

"This napkin got messed up. Take it away and brang me two clean ones, please."

"Two? Okay." He took away the soiled one and quickly returned with two fresh ones. "Is that it?"

"Yeah, thanks." Tige kept one napkin for himself, the other one he unfolded and placed over the top portion of Marvin's meal. "You 'on't mind do you, but I'm ti'ed of that thang wankin' at me."

Tige devoured his steak without further hesitation and took a hefty serving of ice cream and apple pie for dessert.

"I swear I don't know where you put it all."

"Well, I know where I put it in and I know where it comes out, but where it stays between them times, I 'on't know either. We goin' home now?"

"Are you tired?"

"Nope."

"Then let's say we do some sightseeing. They've got a wax museum up the street. Would you like to go?"

"Yeah, I wanna go through everythang they got down heah. Then I wanna go to the movies. You know the one we passed by up on the streets?"

"That was rated X."

"'Snow White' rated X?"

"Oh, *that* one. I thought you meant that other one with all the uh—you know."

"Nawl, man. You need ta keep yo' mind outta the gudder."

"Okay, okay, put your coat on."

"How much you gonna tip George?"

"Since there were only two of us and we didn't even spend fifteen dollars, I think three dollars is fair, don't you?"

"Oh, I would've just gave him a quarder."

"And he would've gave *you* a dirty look. Let's go."

"Bye, George," Tige waved to him on his way out. George smiled and saluted him.

After leaving the restaurant they toured the cobblestone streets of Underground Atlanta, sticking their heads through every door and finally emerging above ground to satisfy Tige's desire to see "Snow White." Marvin couldn't quite keep up with the excited energy Tige possessed, so right after the movie he had to disappoint him slightly by declaring the night over.

Marvin relaxed lazily in bed, dividing his listening between the radio and Tige's voice. Tige was busy telling him key points of the movie he had missed when he went to get popcorn.

Tige adjusted his position against Marvin's side, laying his head on the edge of his chest and resting an arm on his stomach. He hummed along with the song on the radio and drummed his fingers in time on the crystal of Marvin's watch.

Marvin peered at Tige's hand against his. He noticed the contrast of light and dark and marveled to himself at how much he had changed over the years. There had been a time, he recalled, when he would never have let a Negro touch him. His parents had poisoned his mind about the black race when he was young. He was never allowed to play with them or show them any respect—a terrible thing to teach a child. But as he grew older, he decided that *who* he made firends with and showed respect to was his own affair. What his mother and father would think if they saw him now with one of *those* people in his arms.

"What time is that?" Tige asked.

"Fifteen minutes till twelve."

"How can you tell?"

"Because the little hand is on the twelve and the big

hand—if you count here from the twelve, that'll give you fifteen."

"Yeah, I see. I thank I would like me a watch. You got 'nother one somewhere?"

"Afraid not."

"Hey, Marv."

"Yes?"

"How much money you got left?"

"Well, not very much. I probably spent more than I should have. It may take me some time to find a regular job. Why? Did you think of something else you need?"

"Nawl. I was just wond'rin' if we could go someplace else with it. We 'on't have to though if you 'on't wanna. I was just wond'rin' if we could."

"Well, I'd say that depends on what you had in mind."

"I was wond'rin' wouldn't you wanna go ta Six Flags? We ain't gotta though."

"Of course, we don't *have* to. Just a big waste of money. All those special rides they have out there, and live shows and exhibits. Who wants to be bothered with all those childish things?"

"What time we goin'?" Tige asked.

"Soon as the gates open, so get some sleep."

Marvin switched off the radio and the lamp and settled down to sleep.

"Marvin, you turned the light off."

"I thought I did *something* like that."

"It's dark."

"Tige, why are you afraid of the dark?"

"Why are *you* afraid of the light?"

"I'm not afraid, it just bothers me when I'm trying to sleep."

"Well the dark bothers me when *I'm* tryin' ta sleep."

"Oh, there must be a way to make us both

happy.... Oh yeah, I completely forgot. I bought something for you."

Marvin turned the light back on and went to the closet. From his coat he pulled out a bag containing a blue bulb.

"Thought this might come in handy," he said, returning to bed and substituting the blue bulb for the bulb in the lamp. "How's that? Light enough for you?"

"That's pretty. I like that."

"Yeah, it's a lot better than the hundred-watter. Okay, go to sleep."

"Okay."

Tige nestled in close to Marvin and closed his eyes only to find that he wasn't a bit sleepy. He lay quietly for a few moments, hoping that the sandman would overtake him. When he couldn't even get a yawn out, he turned over on his stomach and rose up on his elbows.

"Marvin, you 'sleep?"

"Yes, I am."

"No you ain't—you talked."

"Tige, was there something you wanted?"

"Nawl, I just cain't sleep yet."

"Well have mercy on those of us who can."

"Oh. Sorry.... Hey, Marv, you ever wonder about thangs?"

"Yes, I wonder why you always pick the choicest times to ask questions."

"You wanna go ta sleep, don't cha?"

"I would love to."

"Yeah, well that's what I was wond'rin'. How come people have ta go ta sleep anyway?"

"Because their bodies and minds become exhausted through a long, hard day and they need to rest both of these if they want to continue living a normal and fairly

healthy life—something that you are in danger of losing if
you don't shut up."

"All right, all right. Man, you grouchy."

Tige laid his head down and drummed his fingers on
the bed.

"It's one thang, though, that I wonder 'bout mo'e than
anythang in the world. I wonder a lot 'bout it. . . . Don't
you ever wonder what it feels like ta die?"

"Tige, I asked you not to keep your mind on that."

"Oh, I ain't thankin' about killin' myself ag'in. I 'on't
wanna die. But I was just wond'rin' what it would be like.
Would you feel anythang, would it hurt, or would you just
feel nothin'? Ain't you ever wondered 'bout that?"

"Yes I have."

"But nobody know the answer, do they?"

"Some people think they know. People who believe
in the Bible believe they know the answer."

"That you go ta heaven or hell?"

"Yes."

"Too bad it ain't no way ta know 'head of time. That's
why I didn't go 'head and kill myself. I was sked and I
wa'n't sure 'bout none of that. I was hopin' my mama
would come help me out. Her and yo' wife know what's it
like, don't they? Why do people have ta die? They did my
mama dirty. They made her po' so she'd have ta work all
the time and made her worry and turn gray, and then they
just went and killed her fo' nothin'."

When Tige broke into tears, Marvin pulled him into
his arms.

"Shhh. Look who's still crying for someone after all
these weeks. I thought you were through crying."

"I am . . . just sometimes, I 'member her. . . . Marvin, I
miss her."

"I know you do, Tige, I know you do. But try and

think of it like this. Your mother did have a terrible time of it. I couldn't tell you the reason for it, but everyone's life is different. What we can believe is that since she *was* having such a bad time, then it's just as well that she leave now, so she won't suffer anymore. Maybe she's happy where she is right now, and if she is, then we should be happy for her. The same goes for my wife. I'd like to think of her as keeping a watch over me and having a nice time while she's waiting for me to join her. I may be wrong, but then again, I may be right. No one knows, Tige, so don't worry about it. It'll come soon enough without wondering about it or helping it along. Okay?"

Tige sniffled and nodded.

"Can you go to sleep now?"

"Nawl. Will you tell me a story?"

"No, I have a better idea. Why don't *you* tell *me* one?"

"What you wanna heah?"

"Anything. Use your imagination."

Marvin recalled faintly before dropping off to sleep, a tale of a two-headed dragon, whose heads were at opposite ends, and who could never make up his mind whether to go forward or backward, so it always walked sideways.

"Well," said Marvin as they stopped past the gates of the Six Flags amusement park and gazed over thousands of heads and colorful displays and rides of one kind or another. "Where shall we start?"

"The Scream Machine!" Tige shouted excitedly.

"The Scream Machine," Marvin sighed. "Tell you what. Why don't we start off on something closer to the ground and a lot slower."

"Aw, Marv-v-v. Have you rode it befo'e?"

"No, but I've heard enough about it. That's the one where they give you a red badge of courage if you make it back in one sane piece, and a free pass to the home for the unraveled if you don't. Oh, don't let me stop *you* from going. You're young, you'll make it."

"Aw, Marvin. Come on ride with me, man."

Marvin shook his head. "Those puppydog eyes may work some of the time, but not this time. I'm not letting that thing take ten years off me. You can go on—I'll wait for you."

"Nawl, that's okay," Tige pouted. He lowered his

head and turned back toward the gate.

"Tige, where are you going?"

"Home."

"Home? I thought you wanted to spend the day here."

"I changed my mind. I 'on't wanna now."

"Tige, don't be ridiculous. We've already paid our money. That'd be a stupid waste if we just walked out. Don't you want to go on the rides?"

"Not by myself. I always gotta do thangs all by myself. Come on, Marv-v-v," Tige pleaded, using his wide, dark eyes as sympathy getters. But it wasn't the crocodile tears that looked about to pour any moment that caused Marvin to give in to him. It was the simple fact that now he was looking at Tige through the eyes of a father, and just as he could never deny his own children anything if he could possibly help it, he couldn't see denying Tige either.

Marvin smiled down at him. "You know, you're really getting good at that. Come on, I'm game."

Tige's face immediately lit up gaily even before Marvin could finish talking. He grabbed him by the hand and dragged him off toward the great, white roller coaster.

"Gawd, man!" Tige exclaimed, bedazzled by the heights of the whooping humps of crisscrossing tracks.

"I agree," said Marvin. "Wouldn't you think it'd be better if we waited till we ate first? I think this food would be kind of clumsy holding on to up there."

"You ask me," spoke up a rather pale, overweight gentleman, clutching his stomach as he walked by, "It'll be easier holdin' on to it if you *don't* eat it first." He grumbled off into the crowd.

Tige and Marvin watched him, then looked at each other.

"I thank he's right."

"So do I. I tell you what—when we get in, you hold on to the bag, I'll hold on to you, and let's hope that someone stronger than the both of us will hold on to me."

Marvin survived the Scream Machine and the entire Six Flags outing better than he thought he would have because he found so much pleasure just in watching the excitement on Tige's face. But as the day wore on and the lights of the rides became bright, Tige wasn't smiling as much. He'd been coughing quite a bit, but whenever Marvin questioned him about it, he insisted nothing was wrong or that he had some lint stuck in his throat.

He held onto the tail of Marvin's coat and leaned weakly against him while watching the fireworks in the sky. Finally, he tugged on Marvin's sleeve and hoarsely announced he was ready to go home. They had to ride two buses to get there. Each time, while waiting for the bus to arrive, Tige unbuttoned Marvin's coat and slipped silently beneath. Marvin didn't consider it to be that cold, but Tige obviously did. Every few moments, however, Tige would come out and unzip his own jacket to cool off.

"Tige, is something wrong?" Marvin asked while they were at their downtown bus stop. Tige shook his head and suppressed a cough. "You sure? You're mighty quiet. Don't you feel well?"

He nodded and rezipped his jacket.

"Didn't you have a good time?"

Tige nodded once.

"You don't act like it. Are you tired?"

He nodded once more.

"Well, you've been on the go all day long. You've got a right to be tired. We'll be home soon, then you can go to bed."

Tige stood next to him and leaned his head against his

side. He coughed twice with the congestion in his chest finally becoming audible. Marvin heard it but didn't realize anything was wrong. Tige had been up till late the previous night and had gotten up early that morning; probably he was just exhausted and only needed a good night's rest.

When they were walking the last few blocks to the apartment, Tige lagged a few steps behind. Finally he had to stop and rest against a mailbox. Marvin, after a few feet, found himself walking alone.

"Hey, come on. You've been dragging your feet all the way."

But Tige didn't move away from the mailbox.

"I 'on't feel good," he said in a babyish tone.

Marvin knelt down beside him. "What's wrong? Where don't you feel good?"

"My head hurts."

Marvin pressed a palm against his forehead.

"Feels like you may have a fever. Are you hot or cold?"

"I git hot *and* cold. My throat so'e, too."

"You're coming down with something—maybe the flu. Probably comes from running around in that thin little jacket so much. Come on, let's get you home."

Marvin picked him up and carried him the remaining three blocks and put him promptly to bed.

"I don't have too much around here in the way of medicines. I rarely get sick. I guess I'll just have to go out and get something for you. Think you'll be all right here by yourself?"

Tige nodded feverishly.

"Take it easy. I'll be back soon."

He left him regretfully, and to make up for leaving Tige, he ran a portion of the way to the store. The lines were long at the drugstore, and it took Marvin a few minutes to go through the different drugs and find one that suited Tige's symptoms. It was half an hour before he made it back home.

When he arrived, he stood at the door a second and sighed in relief to see movement from under the covers. He went toward the bed, but was taken aback for a moment by the odor of stale urine.

"I'm sorry I took so long, Tige. How are you feeling?"

"My head still hurts," Tige whispered with a stuffed nose. Marvin felt his forehead.

"I got something for it. Don't worry. This bed..." Marvin grimaced at the odor. "Let's get it cleaned up, okay?"

He lifted Tige's smelly body from the bed along with the top blanket to keep him warm, then laid him across the table. "Stay right there for just a few minutes while I fix the bed."

Tige nodded slightly and through short breaths attempted to explain the obvious.

"I had ta...use the bathroom."

"I know you did," Marvin spoke understandingly as he scrubbed the wet spot with a soaped up towel. "You don't have to explain anything," he said without Tige paying much heed.

"I was too ti'ed ta git up. Where was you, Marvin? I kept waitin' on you ta come."

"I was out getting your medicine. You're going to take it in a few minutes. Let me finish up here first."

Marvin laid a piece of plastic on the mattress and covered it with a fresh sheet. Then he brought a small pan of water to Tige to wash him.

"Let's clean you up and get these things off—they don't smell so good."

Tige allowed himself to be stripped naked and bathed once over. Marvin dried him and gave him one of his T-shirts to wear.

"That feels better, now doesn't it? Nice and clean."

He carried him back to bed and tucked him in.

"Now, what I want you to do for me is take this capsule. Just swallow it down with this water, all right? Come on open up."

Without giving him a chance to object, Marvin plopped the pill into Tige's mouth and forced some water down with it. Tige began to choke, coughing and gasping to clear his throat.

Marvin pulled him quickly over his knee and rapped sharply between his shoulder blades. Tige coughed it up and his breathing began to normalize.

Marvin held him comfortingly and rocked him back and forth. "It's all right, it's all right. I'm sorry. Didn't even ask if you could swallow a capsule. I'm sorry. . . . I see why you don't think you'll live to be twelve—with me around, you won't. I'm not helping you one bit."

He stroked Tige's temple as the child began to fall asleep in his arms. "What am I going to do? I don't know anything about taking care of sick kids. Whenever my kids got sick, Catheryn took care of them. I don't know what she did. All I ever did was bring them games and comic books and move the television set into their rooms. What do I know about . . . I guess I'll just have to learn then, won't I? Okay. I'll give it another try."

He moved to lay Tige down, awakening him with the motion.

"Marvin, where ya goin'?"

"I'm going to have to go back to the store. I'll be right back."

"Don't leave me, Marvin."

"Tige, I have to. I promise, I'll be right back—fifteen minutes, I promise. Just take it easy."

Marvin set out to the drugstore again and returned within the time promised with nearly ten dollars worth of what he thought Tige should have. He fed him orange-flavored aspirin and cherry cough drops, and rubbed his chest with vaporizing cream to ease his breathing.

"Don't worry, you'll feel better in a little while," Marvin told him. "Oh, and while I've got your attention, next time you have to use the bathroom, this," he said holding up a clean mayonnaise jar, "is for liquids. For solids . . . well, just let me know. I'll set it down here beside the bed. Say, you want anything to eat? Are you hungry at all?"

"My stomach hungry, but my mouth ain't."

"Well, maybe later. Get some rest. Need anything, just holler. I'll be here."

It had been three days and Tige's condition hadn't improved much. He still complained of headaches, he couldn't keep his food down, and he couldn't keep from wetting the bed in his sleep.

Marvin was running out of T-shirts, clean sheets, and patience with waking up to the feel of wet spots. He solved the minor problems, though, by letting Tige sleep in the nude, and by waking him at intervals to empty his bladder in the jar. Marvin also made himself a pallet and slept on the floor.

That took care of *his* problems but it didn't do much for Tige. He was still sick with congestion, a fever, coughing, and indigestion.

It worried Marvin. He didn't know if there was something more he should do or if he should simply wait for Tige's virus to pass on its own. He hated to just sit and watch him helplessly. Once, he had to wake him from a nightmare. He was calling for his mama aloud, then telling himself of her death.

"Tige, wake up. You've got to take your medicine."

"I want my mama. Where my mama?" he whined, half asleep.

"Your mama's not here right now. It's me, Marvin. Come on and take your medicine."

Marvin gave him his dose of children's aspirin, which seemed to be highly ineffective. Perhaps what he needed was some strong adult medicine, but Marvin was hesitant about trying some on him because he was so fragile looking and undernourished; he must have lost at least five pounds already in the short time period.

"Feeling any better?" Marvin asked him.

Tige groaned a barely audible response and turned over on his side. Marvin reached over to feel his forehead, thinking how much he wanted to kick himself for not remembering to buy a thermometer. He couldn't tell now if it was his imagination or if Tige's forehead had actually gotten warmer than it was before.

"Tige."

"Mmh?"

"I don't think I can hold off any longer. I'm taking you to Grady."

"I 'on't wanna go no hospital," Tige objected sleepily.

"I'm not asking if you want to go, I'm telling you. You need a doctor, someone who knows what he's doing. All this stuff I've been giving you isn't doing a bit of good. It's probably hurting you a lot more than it's helping."

"I still 'on't wanna go. You ain't got no money ta pay fo' it no way."

"Don't worry about the money. It won't cost me anything. The state'll pay for it."

"You gonna turn me over, ain't cha? I 'on't wanna go ta them people, I rudder die first."

"Stop talking like that, will you! I can't just sit here and watch you suffer like this. You need help."

"I 'on't wanna go ta them people," Tige protested hoarsely.

"Tige . . ."

"*Damn* you! Leave me 'lone, hell just leave me 'lone!" Tige shouted the best he could and moved to the opposite side of the bed.

Marvin propped his head between his hands and shook it gravely. "What am I going to do with you? If I had any sense at all, I'd . . . I don't know, I just don't know anymore. I wish you'd do me a favor," he said crossly over his shoulder. "Either hurry up and get well or just . . . forget it, forget it," he grumbled and left the bed.

He paced around the room while trying to decide what to do, then went back to the bed.

"Okay, let's forget the hospital for a moment. What if I just took you to a doctor's office? They don't ask a lot of questions. They just look at you, give you a shot or a prescription, and send you right back home. We've got to do *something*, Tige."

"You still need money."

"I can get it. I'd have to go out, though. Would you mind being left alone for a while?"

"Don't stay gone all day."

"No, I won't. I'll get back as soon as possible. You take it easy now. I won't be long."

Marvin knew he couldn't earn enough money fast enough by working odd jobs, so his only hope was to try and borrow some. He first tried the bartender of the tavern that he frequented, but Ed had just been robbed two nights before and couldn't afford to lend him even five cents. He thought next of Miss Carrie, but figured that the woman had so many problems of her own, she probably wouldn't be in a position to help him either.

So now he knew what he had to do. He pulled out the slip of paper he'd been hiding from himself in the breast pocket of his coat and looked at it. He would rather rob a bank than go begging to this man, whom he considered his rival. But too many things could go wrong with robbing a bank. This alternative at the moment seemed a lot safer. He headed for the nearest phone booth to make his call. He dialed the number and listened as it rang once and was immediately answered by a bright female voice.

"Good morning, Peachtree Center. May I help you?"

"Yes, I'm trying to locate a Mr. Richard Davis. I believe he may work there."

"Just one moment—I'll check."

"Thank you."

While he was waiting, Marvin pulled out the telephone book and found a host of Richard Davises listed. He closed it and waited for the voice to return over the receiver.

"Sir?"

"Still here."

"Sir, we have three Richard Davises working in this building. Which would you like to speak to? Richard A. Davis, Richard M. Davis, or Richard Davis III?"

Marvin looked at the slip of paper again, which gave no middle initial or special ending.

"Well, I'm not sure which one I want. Which one, if any of them, is black?"

"Sir, in this building, we do not practice racial discrimination."

"I'm glad to hear that, but what I'm getting at is that the Richard Davis I'm looking for *is* black. Now if only one of those gentlemen you mentioned happens to be a black man, then he may be the one I want. Got it?"

"Oh," replied the receptionist in an uncertain tone. "I believe I understand now. Please hold the line."

Marvin waited impatiently, hearing a number of clicks and dial tones, and wondered if it could possibly be so simple to contact Tige's father. If it were, then he wondered if Tige's mother had hated him so much that she didn't even bother to ask him for help when she needed it. Or perhaps she *had* tried, but Tige's father had refused her.

"Sir?"

"Present."

"The one you're looking for is Richard A. Davis. I'll connect you with his office, but would you mind answering a question for me? How did you know he would be black?"

Marvin grinned at her apparent stupidity. "Just a lucky guess."

"Oh. Well I'll connect you."

"Good morning, Marks and Johnson Architects. May I help you?"

"Yes, I'd like to speak to Richard A. Davis, please."

"One moment."

"Hello?"

"Mr. Davis?"

"Yes. Who's callin'?"

"Mr. Davis, you don't know me. My name is Marvin Stewart, and I have something very important to talk to you about."

"Go on."

"Well, not over the phone if you don't mind. It's a personal matter that concerns you. I wonder if we might meet somewhere. It has to be today."

"Uh...well I'm gonna be workin' on half of my lunch hour. If it cain't wait, I guess you could come on up here around twelve."

"All right. You're in the Peachtree Towers, right?"

"Yeah, eighteenth flo', 18-I. Hey, what's this all about? Who are you?"

"I'm Marvin, remember? I'll see you around twelve."

Marvin caught a bus to town and went to one of the towering Peachtree Center buildings, finding that the section he wanted was across the street. He hated elevators, but there was no sense walking up eighteen flights of stairs.

At 18-I, there was a finely furnished entrance with the name of the firm in huge white letters above it. Down the hallway and to the left—as the receptionist directed him— was an open door and a room with several deserted drafting tables. Seated at one of them though, was a young man, absorbed in his work, popping the last bite of something on rye bread into his mouth. He took a sip from a coffee cup, then bent over closely to the work on his drafting table.

Marvin watched him for a moment, taking note of the three-quarters of his face he could see. He concluded that if the man weren't Tige's father, he'd have a tough time in court proving it. The characteristic traits were too dominant to be coincidental.

He was a handsome man in his early thirties, about five-foot-nine, with a small body frame and a neat, two-inch Afro. He took another sip of coffee, pushed his wire-rimmed glasses up on his nose, and finally caught sight of a figure standing in the doorway.

"You're..."

"Marvin Stewart. You're Mr. Davis, I presume."

"Yeah," Richard nodded, and he stood to shake hands. "How'd ya do? Wanna have a seat?"

"Thank you," Marvin responded and took advantage of one of the swiveling stools on wheels that Richard offered him. "I hope I'm not keeping you from your work too much."

"I guess I can spare a few minutes. You said we had somethin' personal to talk about?"

"Yes. It seems that we have one common denominator."

"Is that a fact? And what's that?"

"It's not a what, it's a who—Tige Jackson."

"And who's Tige Jackson?"

"Has it been so long that you don't remember your own son?"

Richard froze momentarily and eyed him with the same suspicious look Tige would have had.

"I don't have a son," he stated bluntly.

"Oh, don't you?"

"I've got three children—they're all girls."

"All girls. Three are all you have?"

Richard nodded once.

"Well, exactly when was it you started counting?"

"Hey, just who are you anyway?" Richard began to show his temper. "What business is it of yo's?"

"Actually, I'm nobody to be concerned about. I'm just the guy in the middle. I've been sort of a guardian to Tige since his mother died."

Marvin noticed a definite reaction in the other man's eyes, though Richard attempted to hide it.

"Oh, I guess I should have told you that first. Miss Jackson passed on a couple of days before Thanksgiving. She was quite penniless, and she had no other relatives except for Tige. Anyway, I saw no harm in keeping him myself awhile."

"Why didn't you just dump him in an orphanage and be done with it?" Richard said crossly.

"Well now that I see he has a perfectly good father..."

"I am *not* that boy's father! Not anymo'e." Richard spoke with his teeth clenched and with the same indentation over his brow as Tige.

"Now I told Vanessa when she was pregnant with him to get herself an abortion. I was gonna pay for it. But no, she was too afraid. And when that kid was bo'n, I told her to put him up for adoption. But no, that was her baby and she wasn't giving him away to strangers. Now it's not my fault she held on to him."

"That doesn't matter, Mr. Davis. He's still your son."

"But he's not my responsibility. I am not paying for that woman's mistakes! Listen..." he began in a gentler tone. "I have a wife and three daughters. Tige is two months younger than my oldest girl. How am I going to explain that to people—to *them?* Now, I love my wife. I couldn't make Vanessa understand that. It was just a little fling with her. It didn't mean anythang. But she wanted me to give up my wife and future just for her. I said no, so she cussed me out, spit in my face, and told me to get the hell on, and that's *just* what I did."

"Well, I guess I can see your point somewhat. Actually, though, I didn't come to try and hand him back to you. Considering you never cared for him before, I really didn't expect you to be overjoyed at the chance to have him now. You see, Mr. Davis, I don't care two cents about you personally *or* your family or what they would think. I'm not interested in that at all. My only concern is Tige. I wouldn't have come to you at all if I didn't *have* to. But so far you're my only good candidate for help."

"Help? What kind of help?"

"Tige is ill. He has a very bad virus and he's dead set

against being admitted to a hospital because the first thing that would happen would be for them to call in somebody from child welfare and he'd end up in the state's custody."

"And what's so wrong with that? That's where he should be anyway. You could probably be arrested for holdin' on to him."

"And maybe his father could be arrested for nonsupport. How do you think your family would react to *that*?"

"What is it you want?"

"As I was saying, he's sick and if I could just have a doctor look at him, give him a shot or prescription, I'm pretty sure I could handle it from there. But the trouble is that I'm lacking funds. I don't even have enough for cabfare, so if you could just spare a little something— anything at all."

Richard snickered and shook his head. "You must take me for a fool, don't you? You really expect me to believe that. You come walking in from nowhere—I don't even know you—and you expect me to just hand you some money because you ask me to. You are crazy as hell."

"Mr. Davis, if you don't believe me, all you have to do is come home with me and see for yourself."

Richard turned in his chair and thought it over a few seconds.

"What's the matter?" Marvin asked. "Afraid I may be telling the truth? Are you so afraid of a little boy?"

"I'm not afraid of *nothin'*."

"Then come with me."

"I'm not goin' *nowhere*. For all I know, you may be just a quack who goes around diggin' up things about people, then tries to blackmail 'em. But it's not gonna work with me because I don't play that shit. Now I'm gonna be good enough to pretend you never came in here, but if you wanna try and play games with me, I'll be glad to take you on. So why don't you just turn around and walk out that do'."

"Would you rather I bring him to you?"

"I rather you get yo' behind out that do' before I call a security guard to come and *throw* you out."

Marvin could see that there was no use in pleading with him. He hung his head in despair, then rose and started to leave. He stopped before reaching the door and turned around for a few last words.

"Just one more thing, Mr. Davis, if I may. Those three girls of yours—are you happy with them?"

"What's that suppose to mean?"

"I was just asking if you were happy with them. Are they exactly what you and your wife planned and hoped for? I ask that because I've been a father also—correction—I *am* a father also. My children aren't anything like what I expected when my wife and I started a family. I wasn't truly happy with them most of the time, but I never let that stop me from caring for them—from giving them a decent home to grow up in.

"Let me tell you something, Mr. Davis. Have you any idea what your son was about to do when I first met him? He was sitting on a bench in the park trying to decide the best way to kill himself. Can you imagine an eleven-year-old kid with a knife against his wrist ready to call it quits? Of course that was pretty understandable then. That was the day he lost his mother. He didn't think he had anything to live for, until I convinced him he did. But even so, he still doesn't feel he'll ever amount to anything. He doesn't even want to try. He feels he won't even live to see twelve. Or that if he does grow up, he won't be like regular people. He thinks he'll just rot away year by year unless, of course, he decides to kill himself again and there's no one to stop him."

Marvin shook his head pityingly. "I'll tell you, I have never in my life met anyone like that before, Mr. Davis— someone so young who doesn't feel his life is worth living or making something better of. And *you!*" Marvin raised his voice and slapped his hand down on a nearby table. "I have never met anyone like you either. Are you so selfish, so damned high and mighty, so . . . *scared* of what people would say or think that you have to brush him off as someone else's mistake? What kind of man are you? *Are you a man?* Because no matter how many times you deny it or how much you try to hide it, he's *still* your little bastard!"

Richard sat, unemotionally moved, then clapped his hands together three times. "You put on a good act, alright, but the show's over and I *don't* want an encore. Get out."

Marvin managed to control his temper.

"Thank you for your *precious* time. Good day."

He returned home and found Tige asleep. He started to pull the covers up around him but found that the sheets were wringing wet with sweat.

"Oh great," he sighed. He went into the bathroom to get one of the ones he had washed earlier. He took his coat to wrap Tige in to keep him from getting a chill while he changed the linen. But he found something strange in Tige's reaction to being moved. The strange thing was that there was *no* reaction at all. Usually he'd stir and wake if only for a second. But now his body was limp, his head rolled and his arms dangled out of control. Marvin laid him back down for a moment to check him.

"Tige? Tige!" He shook him gently to try and wake him. When he showed no signs of waking, Marvin began to get nervous.

"Come on, Tige. Wake up, wake up." He felt for his pulse. It was so weak he could hardly detect it. "Oh, God, no! Got to get you some help."

He hastily finished wrapping him up in his coat, scooped him up in his arms and hurried out the door. He moved down the stairs as quickly as possible, then stopped at the bottom of them to figure out which way he should go. He saw cars driving by, so he tried to flag one down. When the first few past him by, he stood in the middle of the road to force the next one to stop.

"What are you—crazy?" the man driving it yelled at him.

"Please, I need help! I have to get him to a hospital. He's very sick."

The snarling frown on the man's face vanished when he noticed the bundle in Marvin's arms. Then he reached behind himself to unlock the rear door.

"Get in."

Marvin hurried into the back seat, using up all available space. A little girl about six years old was in the front seat and had turned around to stare at him.

"I think Grady's the closest," said the man. "Is that all right?"

"Yeah, that'll be fine."

"What's wrong with him?"

"I don't know. It started out as a cold, I think. But now I don't know. It's just gotten worse. Would you mind stepping on it a little?"

"Sure. I'll get you there, don't worry."

Marvin secured the collar of the coat about Tige's neck and felt for his pulse again. It was becoming harder to find. Marvin looked heavenward and closed his eyes to pray. The little girl who'd been staring at him silently finally found the courage to speak.

"Whose little bo-oy is he?"

Marvin opened his eyes and glanced at her.

"He's mine," he answered with tears attempting to cut off his speech.

"But you're white and he's bla-ack," she pointed out.

Marvin shrugged his shoulders slightly. "Guess I hadn't noticed."

She was about to make another comment when the man told her to turn around and be quiet. The silence gave Marvin a chance to finish his prayer.

It only took five minutes to get to the hospital but naturally it seemed like hours. Marvin quickly thanked the driver, hurried Tige through the doors, and stopped the first person in white he saw. The nurse's reaction immediately was to check Tige's pupils and pulse while Marvin stammered out a plea for help.

"I can't get him to wake up. Please, he needs a doctor."

"Bring him this way," she told him, while leading the way to an emergency room. She instructed him to lay Tige on the table and made a phone call for a doctor to report promptly to the room. When she started to pull Tige's coat off, Marvin felt he should explain why Tige was naked beneath it.

"I didn't have time to dress him," he said. "He kept wetting the bed—that's why he isn't wearing anything."

"Yes sir, there's no need to explain." She handed him the coat and covered Tige with a sheet. Then she pulled out a tablet and pencil from her pocket. "The doctor will be right in. Now I need to get some information if you can help me out sir. What is his name?"

"Yes. His name is uh . . . uh . . . *Tige*. T-i-g-e Jackson."

"How long has he been like this?"

"Unconscious? I'm not sure. An hour, maybe more or less. I'm not sure. What's taking the doctor so long?"

"He's on his way," she assured him calmly. She went

to the door and looked out. "Kilpatrick," Marvin heard her call out. Kilpatrick, a young Oriental nurse, appeared at the door. "Take this gentleman to admittance and start a file on Tige Jackson."

"Okay. Sir, would you follow me please?"

A doctor appeared then and headed straight for Tige. Marvin would have liked to stay but the young nurse tugging on his arm was still insisting that he go with her. He went along with her and answered her questions. When asked about Tige's parents, Marvin froze.

"I said I need to have his parents' names," she repeated.

"He...uh...he doesn't have any."

"Oh, I see. I don't suppose you're related to him in any way?"

"I was *going* to adopt him, but, well he got sick."

"So actually, he's an orphan?"

"Yes. I picked him up off the streets. What will you do with him?"

"Nothing at the moment. But if he *is* without any living relatives, then we will have to contact the State Welfare Board so that when he's better, they can find somewhere to place him. There are no living relatives that you know of?"

"No," Marvin answered.

When she had finished her interrogation, she told him where to wait and promised to keep him posted on Tige's condition. He waited on edge for nearly an hour before a doctor—the same one as before—came to see him.

"Mr. Stewart? I'm Dr. Ross."

"How is he?"

"As well as can be expected. He's in a coma now."

"Coma? But what happened? What's wrong with him?"

"He has a very bad case of pneumonia."

"Oh no!"

"Needless to say, pneumonia is bad enough for someone big and strong like yourself, but with him—he's small and suffering from malnutrition—the odds aren't good. I'm sorry to say I've done all that I can for him. It's not up to me anymore."

"Are you saying that he's . . . dying?"

"I'm saying there's that possibility. Either he wakes from the coma—and there's no way of predicting when—or he won't wake at all. All we can do is pray and hope someone hears. I'm sorry."

Marvin felt a pain starting up in the center of his chest, and tears began to well in his eyes. "Would it have made a big difference if I had brought him in sooner?"

"Pneumonia is a tricky disease. It could kill some people no matter how soon they're treated. I can't say definitely that we could have prevented him from getting worse, but don't blame yourself if that's what you have in mind. It won't help him any, and it certainly won't help you. Well, just thought I'd keep you informed—I'll let you know later when you can see him, alright?"

"Yes, thank you."

Marvin walked around in a daze. He wasn't going to cry because that only meant he was committing himself to the fact that Tige would die. He wouldn't let himself think that. He looked through his pockets to find some change for a cup of coffee, though doubting that it would calm his nerves. He felt a piece of paper, but thinking that it was only a store receipt or a bus transfer, he started to ball it up and throw it away. Then suddenly it occurred to him what it was. He stared at the name and number contemplating whether or not to call. As his father—unwilling or not—Richard had the right to know that his small worry might soon be over. He used the dime to make the call. After the preliminaries with the receptionist, Richard's voice came on.

"Hello?"

Marvin held his tongue for a moment while forming the words he wanted to use.

"Hello?" Richard repeated.

"Mr. Davis, this is Marvin Stewart again."

"What do *you* want? You know what I told you befo'e."

"No, I didn't call for money. I just called to let you know that your little whatchamacallit is at Grady Memorial. He has pneumonia and may not make it. I doubt if it really means anything to you. Just a little piece of news I thought I might pass along. Oh, by the way, I didn't tell them that you were his father, so if he *should* die, the state will be paying for the funeral. You won't have to be bothered. And you won't be hearing from me again either. Goodbye."

He hung up on him, then went to stand outside Tige's room, waiting for a chance to see him. When his chance came, he went in quietly. Tige was in an oxygen tent, with various tubes and needles attached to his nose, mouth, and arms; a cardiograph machine was monitoring his heartbeat. Marvin watched the steady pattern it drew over and over, fearfully expecting it to stop at any second.

"Tige," he called out softly, hoping to wake him with his voice. He got no response. "Poor Tige. Why does everything always have to happen to you? Don't die on me, son, please don't. Just pull through for me. I'll make it all worth your while. I promise I will. I'll see to it you get the best of everything. You'll never have to go without again. I promise. Just don't . . . don't die."

He fought back the tears and sought out a chair near the door. He kept his eyes open for any movement on the bed and his ears tuned to the beeping of the cardiograph. Nothing happened for nearly an hour. Then Richard walked in.

Richard headed straight for the bed, stopping a few feet from it as if he wasn't sure what he wanted to do. Finally he stepped closer and looked through the clear vinyl at his son. He gazed at him for a few moments longer, then bowed his head and turned slowly away. When he started for the door, he saw Marvin sitting there quietly watching him.

"Concerned or curious?" Marvin asked, keeping his seat.

"A little of both," Richard answered, glancing back at Tige. "He looks so . . . so helpless. Would it have helped if I'd given you the money?"

"No. It's just one of those things. Either he wakes or he doesn't. It's all up to him and the Man upstairs now. All we can do is wait."

Richard walked back over timidly to take another peek at Tige. "Even with the way he looks now, you can tell he favors me, can't you? The last time I saw him he was only two. Nine years. Most of the time I never thought about him. But sometimes little memories would sneak up on me and I'd wonder about him."

"But never enough to go find out."

"No, not as long as Vanessa was around."

Richard paused and stepped out of the way when a nurse came into the room to check Tige's vital signs. There was nothing new to report.

"Well," said Richard. "Looks like we're gonna be here for a while. Can I buy you a cup of coffee?"

Marvin was surprised by the offer, but after a longing glance at Tige, he rose slowly from the chair and went along with Richard.

"You say you've been takin' care of him since Thanksgivin'?" Richard asked while seated across the table from Marvin in the hospital cafeteria.

"Yes. But obviously I didn't do too good a job of it. I let a little kid talk me out of doing what I knew I should have done."

"But you did yo' best. Most folks wouldn't bother. I wish I could've known about it sooner."

"When I talked to you earlier, it seemed you were whistling a different tune."

"Yeah, I know. It was just talk. I guess because it was so much of a shock—you know so all of a sudden. I've had some time to think about it now. And I know I want my son to live. And I know I want to take him home with me."

Marvin quickly took a sip of his coffee. He wanted to blurt out that Tige belonged to him and that he'd do anything to keep him. But managed to keep silent as Richard continued.

"You see, Vanessa is what stood in the way. She could never git me to marry her, so takin' Tige away from me was her way of getting even. I bet she's told him all sorts of lies about me. But I don't care *what* she's told him. I'd like to prove to him myself what his old man is really like. Now I have the chance. Maybe."

"Yes, maybe. You have a wife and three daughters if I recall correctly. What will they think about your extracurricular activities?"

"I guess I'll find out. My wife is pretty understanding about things. She loves me. She's stood beside me through a lot of hard times. I'm bankin' that she won't change on me all of a sudden."

"But what if she should?"

"No, I don't think so. I owe that boy a lot. I want to try and make it up to him. Oh, and I want to thank you for doing what you have for him. I'm willing to pay you for yo' troubles."

"That's not necessary. I didn't do it for money."

"Why *did* you do it?"

"I don't know. It's like asking someone who climbed a mountain why he did it."

"Because it was there?"

"Yes, and also because it looked pretty lonely out there all by itself."

They finished their coffee without saying much more to each other. But instead of returning to Tige's room, they went into the waiting room. Marvin stretched out on a couch and fell asleep only seconds after closing his eyes. Richard paced the floor and looked out the window from time to time while rehearsing all the speeches he was planning to give to his wife and children and to Tige when the time arrived. Every once and awhile he'd glance at his watch and get the feeling that the speeches wouldn't be necessary and that, instead, he would have to think about funeral arrangements.

"Is there someone here named Marvin?" a nurse appeared at the door and asked. Richard pointed a finger to the man on the couch, then went to wake him.

"Hey, Stewart, wake up. Someone wants you."

"Mmm? What—what?"

"You're Marvin?" the nurse asked.

"Yes, yes. What is it?"

"Are you familiar with Tige Jackson?"

"Yes. Do you have news? Is he..."

"Yes, he is. We've already taken down the oxygen tent. He won't be needing it anymore. You can see him now if you like."

"I can—you mean he's *alive?*"

"Of course. What did you think I meant? He's been calling for you."

Both Marvin and Richard broke into large grins of relief. Marvin read the nurse's nametag, then grabbed her face and gave her a big smack on the cheek.

"Thank you, Mrs. Morgan, I love you!"

He dashed out with Richard following closely. The doctor was just coming out of Tige's room when they arrived.

"Oh, I'm glad you're here," he spoke to Marvin. "Looks like your little friend is going to make it all right. He's small, but he's tough." Then he noticed Richard. "Are you any relation?"

"Yes, I'm his father."

"But I thought..."

"It's a long story," Richard told him.

"Well, I'd like to hear it. After you've seen him, of course. But please don't excite him or upset him any. I'll talk to you later."

"All right. Thank you."

Marvin walked in with Richard close behind and stopped beside Tige's bedside. The boy's eyes were closed. Marvin whispered.

"Hey there, Tiger."

Tige opened his eyes slowly and focused on him.

"How you feeling?"

"Ti'ed," Tige spoke, his voice hoarse and whispery.

"You gave me a scare there for awhile, but you're going to be all right."

"This is a hospital?"

"Yes. I knew how you felt about it, but there was nothing left to do. I had to. But don't worry about someone coming to take you away from me. You know how I sometimes come up with these brilliant lies to get both our tails out of trouble? Well, I did it again. I told them that your parents are out of the country and I was your official baby-sitter."

"They believe that?"

"Well, all I had to convince was this one nurse who blushes everytime I smile at her. A little sweet talk can work miracles. So now you're in my custody and when you're well, we can walk right out the door together. You like that?"

"Yeah, that's good. Oh-h-h-h. What's all this shit they got stuck up my nose?"

"Watch your language."

"Oh. I meant *stuff*."

"That stuff is just something to help you. Anytime they want to stick something up you, you let them because it's all to get you well."

"Okay, okay. Who he?" Tige asked, just now taking notice of Richard. Richard was prepared to be introduced, and Marvin was about to do it, when he suddenly changed his mind.

"He's...uh...a doctor. He was a bit curious about you and just wanted to drop in." Richard was about to object but Marvin signaled to him not to say anything. "Thank you for your concern," he said to him. "I know you have to go, so I'll talk to you later." Marvin gave him a gentle shove and after a few seconds more, Richard took the hint.

"Yeah, I'll probably see you outside later." Then he left the two alone.

"Hey, Marv."

"Yes?"

"You said you was worried 'bout me?"

"Yeah, a little."

"Was you sked I was gonna die?"

"Well, you *were* pretty sick. I was a little scared."

"Aw man. Don't cha know . . . I wouldn't leave you."

Marvin smiled and nodded. "I guess I should've known better," he said. Then he got an irresistible urge to do something he'd never done before. Being careful of Tige's medical attachments, he bent down and placed a kiss on his forehead.

"Man-n-n, what's wrong with you?" Tige complained. "I'm a boy. You ain't 'pose ta kiss me."

"Forgive me. I lost my head."

"Come heah."

"What is it?"

"Come down." Tige's voice was almost inaudible, so Marvin lowered his ear down to him. Tige touched his lips against the side of his face.

"Don't tell nobody I did that," he warned afterward.

"Don't worry, I won't." Marvin watched as Tige's eyes fluttered drowsily. "Sleepy?"

"A li'l'. You gonna stay with me?"

"I'll stay for awhile, then I think I'll go home and get some rest. I'll be back tomorrow though. You'll be all right, won't you?"

"Yeah. Hey, don't you wanna tell me a story be'fo'e ya go?"

"Sure. I know a good one. Once upon a time there

lived this fairly good-looking middle-aged man who met this little boy that had been dipped in chocolate...."

Tige's eyelids lowered a final time. Marvin pulled the covers up and tucked them around him, then gave Tige another kiss.

"And they lived happily ever after. Take it easy, partner, I'll see you later."

Richard was waiting down the hall from Tige's room.

"All right, now what was that all about?" he asked with a hint of anger. "Why didn't you tell him who I really was?"

"For one very good reason, Mr. Davis. You heard what the doctor said. We're not to excite him or upset him. Now the only good thing Tige has been told about you was that you were long gone. Just to find out that you're around is one thing, but to know that you want to take him away from ... that you want to take him, there's no telling what kind of effect it could have. In the condition he's in now, I just didn't want to chance it."

Richard nodded. "Yeah, I guess you're right. Well, what do you suggest? How about if I just hang around pretending to be a doctor or whatever and he can start getting used to me. And once he gets to like me, that's when I can tell him who I am."

"No, no I don't think so."

"Why not?"

"Well, for one thing, if he should ever ask you any medical questions—which I can promise you he will—and you can't answer them, he'll know you aren't a doctor. And secondly, you look too much like him for it to be a coincidence. I guarantee, eventually he'll notice."

"Yeah. Well, you got any bright ideas since you shot down all mine?"

"I suggest we take it slow. We should wait until he's completely recovered and there's no chance of a relapse. As soon as he's well enough to leave the hospital, I think it would be best if he came home with me."

"With you, huh?"

"Yes. He's used to me. You saw for yourself that's what he expects anyway. So we go along with it. That way, I can start throwing hints casually and ease the truth out gently to keep from shocking him. That's the way I see it. If you have anything better . . ."

"No, no. You just made me realize something anyway. He needs time to get use to the idea of *me*, my family will need time to get used to the idea of *him*. I still haven't figured out how I'm going to tell them. They'll need time to adjust and get ready. So will I, for that matter. Guess maybe you *should* hold on to him for awhile. Don't want to paint myself into a corner just yet. Let's see . . . he'll be here for a week or two, won't he?"

"Possibly."

"Then about a week with you. That should be enough time. Okay, we'll do it yo' way."

"And you won't have to worry about getting in touch with me. I'll get in touch with you when the time is right."

"Okay, you'll need my home phone number, or do you already have it?"

"No, I don't."

Richard took out a pen and searched for a slip of paper. He hit upon his checkbook and pulled it out.

"Well, while I'm at it . . . I want you to have this."

He wrote out an amount for one-hundred dollars and gave it to Marvin.

"I told you before this wasn't necessary."

"You also said you didn't have any money, so how were you expecting to take care of my son when he got out?"

"It won't take this much."

"Well whatever you don't use, you can give to him as a going away present. Take it. My address is on there, so you can copy it before you cash it. All right?"

"All right. Now I think we should let someone around here in on our deal."

"Yeah, that's right. You know something funny? I don't know why, but I feel like a brand new father."

"Mr. Davis, I hate to burst your bubble, but have you considered the fact that Tige may not take to you at all?"

"Yeah, I considered. He may hate my guts—I know that. But I'd never forgive myself if I didn't at least *try* to be a real daddy to him. You can understand that, can't you?"

"Yes, I'm afraid I can. Well, shall we go talk to someone?"

"After you."

Tige's stay in the hospital lasted ten days. When he started complaining about the skimpy diet they had him on and demanded some *real* food, and then began using obscene language and hand gestures against a particular nurse he disliked, everyone felt it was time he was released.

Marvin had proven his ability as a convincing liar, so Tige still accepted the story he had told him. Richard took full responsibility for signing him out and paying his bill, but Tige never knew about it. There were a lot of questions he could have asked on the subject, but he decided to leave well enough alone. As long as he was going back home with Marvin and no one else was taking him, there seemed no reason to doubt Marvin's word.

At home, Tige came running out of the bathroom and bounded onto the bed.

"Now you know what the doctor told you," said Marvin. "No overexertion."

"Yeah, but he didn't tell me what he was talkin' 'bout."

"He meant no running around and jumping up and down. You'll need a lot of bed rest."

"*Bed rest?* I'm already saddle so'e."

"Do you want to go back to the hospital?"

"Nope."

"Then you do what I tell you, you hear."

"Yeah, yeah. Hey, you know them hospitals got po'table compact toilet stools?"

"Yes, they're called bedpans."

"Yeah, that's right. Why them doctors always gotta shine a light in yo' eyes?"

"Tige, not now. I have a lot on my mind."

"Like what?"

"It's too much to talk about, not just yet anyway. It concerns both of us, but I need time to work things out. You'll just have to be patient. I promise things'll work out okay. You trust me, don't you?"

Tige tucked his bottom lip under his top and nodded.

"Why don't you just go to bed now."

"Okay. Goodnight, Marvin."

"Goodnight."

Marvin lay in bed for two hours sipping Scotch and concentrating on his problems. He finished his drink and got up for a refill, which he took with him to the chair in front of the heater. He sat down before the gas flames to think some more. He'd never win custody of Tige now that his father wanted him. He had known he would have a battle on his hands just being the wrong color; now it was hopeless.

The facts were clear and simple—he wasn't fit to take care of a child. It was his stupidity and neglect that had caused Tige to become so ill. Even if he had a job and was able to buy him things and send him to school, there would still be something wrong with it. He kept imagining himself dead on the streets with Tige waiting at home for him—and waiting and waiting. If he should die, it could mean the breaking point for Tige. At least with Richard's family, there would still be others left to fall back on. He wouldn't feel as lost and hopeless with others to lean on.

Richard had so much he could offer, and not only money. Marvin could see that he was a man of compassion and sincerity. Tige could learn to love him easily. There was only one answer. He knew what he had to do, but he just couldn't bring himself to go into action. He slumped back in his chair and stared through the semidarkness at the bright yellow flames of the heater, concentrating on the little bumps of the grates as they flared up orange and white.

Motion caught his eye as Tige, wrapped in his jacket, passed by him on the way to the bathroom. He came out a minute later, walked a half circle around Marvin, studying him carefully, then came to a halt behind him and placed a hand on his shoulder.

"What you doin' up, Marvin? You sick?"

"No. Just a little restless. You can't pay much attention to us old folks. We get senile and do all sorts of things in the middle of the night."

Tige took a lock of Marvin's hair and placed it into the position he thought it should go.

"I know," he said softly. "You was thankin', wa'n't ya? My mama used ta git up in the middle of the night and walk 'round and thank. She be worrin' about money and bills and how we gonna git this and that . . . and sometimes about me. If I ever grow up, I ain't never gonna have no chillun that I have ta sit and worry over."

"*If* you grow up? Why do you say things like that? Kids usually say, '*when* I grow up,' not 'if I ever.' You don't think you'll live that long—why?"

Tige shrugged his shoulders. "I 'on't know. Just sometimes I feel that way. Like when you git mad at me and I thank you gonna kick me out; I just feel like I ain't got nothin' and nobody and I'll have ta make it on my own. I ain't sho I can do that though. Either I die of somethin' or I'll just have ta grow up ta be like them guys on the co'ner—sleep in old cars, and beg fo' money on the streets, and make fires in the trash cans ta keep wa'm.... They prob'bly all started out like me.... Marvin, you thankin' about kickin' me out? I know I been a lotta trouble—if you ti'ed of me, I'll understand."

"Hey-y-y, come here."

Marvin took him by the hand and guided him around to his lap.

"Now, what was that about be being tired of you? What kind of talk is that? Mm?"

Tige shrugged his shoulders bashfully. "I 'on't know," he said softly. "I guess 'cause you acted like somethin' wrong. You didn't hardly say nothin' ta me tonight. And now you drankin' ag'in."

"Oh, that. To tell you the truth, I'm feeling just a little shaken up. Would you believe I nearly fell off a roof the other day?"

"Ooh. I guess that'd scare the shoot outta me too. I'm glad you didn't git hurt."

"So am I."

"You comin' back ta bed?"

"In a little while. You run on back though."

"Do I have ta? I wanna stay heah awhile."

Marvin smiled lightly and nodded once.

Tige squirmed in his lap to make himself comfortable beneath Marvin's chin and allowed his head to rise and fall with the man's rhythmic breathing. He felt so warm and safe as a huge thumb wiped smoothly across his cheek twice, then dropped to his shoulder and stayed there.

The room was quiet and soothing. From the inside of

his eyes, Tige could see himself back home in his old apartment—the room softly lit and his mother stroking his temple ever so gently. His head lay on her lap or against the side of her bosom beneath her arm. She would sit and hum religious songs, tapping her foot and patting her knee in rhythm. It reminded Tige of slavery movies. The young Negro woman with calloused hands and not much desire left in her body sung to her child to keep him from being frightened of the next morning. His mother never really complained. She took things quite as they were, never believing that there could be anything different. She was right. It was sad to have her work her life away with nothing to show for it. Just wasted away miserably until she could go on no longer. Tige shuddered as the thought of her dead face returned in his memory.

"What's wrong?" Marvin's voice came from a thousand miles away. "Tige?"

"Nothin'," Tige answered quickly.

"Nothing? You sure?"

"Uh huh."

Marvin didn't question him anymore. He patted his arm and remained quiet.

"It ain't fair, Marvin," Tige stated after a long silence.

"What ain't—isn't?"

"How some people got a whole lotta money and others ain't got nothin'. All them rich people buyin' thousand-dollar cars and the po' people ain't hardly got nowhere ta live. How come it's like that? That ain't fair."

"I know it isn't fair. I don't know why it's like that, no. It just is. There's been a class of rich and poor about as long as the world's been going. Not all rich people are born rich. They fight the world to get that way. A lot of people just don't know how to fight that way. They give up too soon and they stay poor. Then they pass it on to their children. If those children can't learn to fight their way to the top, then they can easily sink to the very bottom. Me, I'm an ex-fighter, retired from the ring. What do you plan on being?"

"Man, I'm a loser. I been fightin' since the day I was bo'n and still ain't got nowhere yet."

He sighed heavily, then began counting his fingers, but ran into a bit of difficulty and gave up.

"How long I got ta go ta be twen'y-one?"

"You're eleven—add ten years to it."

"Shit! 'Scuse me."

"You're excused."

"That's a long time, Marv. I wish I was already dare. I wish I was all growed up and had a good job and makin' me some money."

"What would you do with all that fantastic salary?"

"Man, I'd buy me everythang I ever wanted—a house, and a car, and pretty furniture..."

"Wouldn't you need someone to share that with? A young lady?"

"Talkin' 'bout a wife? I 'on't know, maybe. If I could find me a pretty one—real nice. Wouldn't have no chillun though, 'less I was sure I could affo'd 'em. Man, that's just dreams though. That ain't never gonna happen."

"It *could*," said Marvin.

"How could it?"

"If you'd let someone else take care of you. Someone who could provide you with the chance to have a better future. Maybe someone out there might like to adopt you."

"Aw man, who gonna be 'doptin' me? You tell me that."

"You'll never know, Tige. A lot of people would like a nice kid like you."

Tige snickered meaninglessly. "Man, you gotta be kiddin'. Marv, you know me. I cuss, I steal, I talk back at people, I'm dumb, I ain't got no manners . . . shoot man, you dreamin'."

"You're the one who's dreaming, Tige. You're so busy thinking about your bad points, you forget to even consider your good ones. You're really not quite the monster you think you are, you know. Just think about yourself. Remember the way you sounded off on the subject of whitey?—as if you hated the entire white race. But if that's so, then what are you doing here? I'm just as white as they come. See, it just goes to show that you aren't full of hate.

"You're thoughtful, too, and very generous—the way you let me have your hamburger that first night, and the way you always save something for me whenever we go out and get food. And the Christmas present—you used your own money to buy me something, not knowing that I would give you something in return. Once you realize it, Tige, you're not a *bad* kid. You're a good kid growing up in a lousy situation. You're sweet and you don't even know it."

Tige turned up a corner of his mouth and glanced sideway at Marvin.

"It's true," Marvin smiled. "Now tell me," he said, taking hold of Tige's chin and turning it toward himself. "What motherly-type lady could pass up those two big beautiful eclipses? How could she resist them?"

"Easy, if I wo'e dark shades."

"Yeah." Marvin let go of his chin and sighed.

"But you do see what I'm getting at, don't you? You're not a terrible person, and if you gave it a chance, you probably *could* become adopted."

Tige dropped his eyes. The last few words had

deadened him. He took his position against Marvin's chest again, wrapped his arms about the man's waist, and clasped his hands together in back.

"Must have said the wrong thing, huh? Tige . . . Tige, I am the biggest fool who ever lived. Everything I try to do just blows up in my face. I have something I have to tell you. I just don't know exactly how to put it."

Marvin wrapped his arms around Tige tightly, not allowing him to object or move. Tige thought he was playing a game at first. He tried to wiggle loose, only he couldn't. The hold was too strong. Marvin forced the boy's head down on his shoulder and rocked him slowly.

It finally occurred to Tige that it wasn't a game of any kind, and his mind raced, trying to read what was happening. The last time someone had held him this way, it was Vanessa, the night before she died. She knew she was going to die, and that had been her silent way of saying goodbye. Now Marvin was using it.

"Marv?"

"Shh. Not now," Marvin whispered, his voice cracking. He was trying hard not to cry.

Tige tightened his arms around his neck to comfort him. He could feel Marvin's heart thumping and his body trembling with silenced sniffles. It made Tige want to cry also.

They clung together a few seconds more before Marvin found the strength to speak.

"Do . . . do me a favor. Go back to bed. I have to go out."

He released him and turned away quickly to hide his face.

"Marvin?"

"I have to make a phone call. I'll be back later," Marvin said in leaving.

Tige stared sadly at the closing door, wondering who Marvin could possibly have to call. He was probably going out to get loaded. And in that case, Tige didn't want to be awake when he returned. He went to bed, praying that none of his fears would come true.

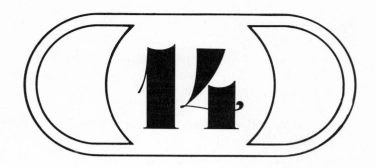

"Hey, sleepyhead—wake up. You plan on spending all day in bed?"

Tige wiped the sleep from his eyes and made it out of bed. Marvin was chipper, humming along with the radio, and setting breakfast on the table. Tige went along with his good mood. Maybe what he thought last night wasn't what it appeared to be. Marvin seemed perfectly normal now. They talked over breakfast—ignoring last night's episode—decided it was too early to go anywhere, and ended up working on the puzzle.

"We almost through with this, ain't we?" Tige queried while piecing together parts of the sky.

"Almost," Marvin answered.

"I sho hope ain't none missin'. Did you ever count it ta make sure it was a thousand?"

"Once—only I came up with a thousand and eight. I believe I counted twice somewhere along the line."

Tige pieced together several more consecutive pieces.

"All-l-l-l right! I'm hot now. Look at that. Hey, is we

[193]

gonna glue this on cardboa'd and hang it on the wall? ... Marv? Hey."

"Huh? Sorry, I wasn't listening. Did you say something?"

"Nope. I was just sangin'."

"Oh."

Tige watched as Marvin daydreamingly put two totally different colored pieces together, not noticing that they didn't fit after he'd done it.

"Hey, Marv. Mar-r-rvin-n-n-n."

Tige snapped his fingers in front of Marvin's face at last to get his attention.

"What? You say something?"

"Yeah. Where was you just now?"

"Nowhere—I mean—I was thinking about the puzzle."

"You lyin'. What's a madder, Marv?"

Marvin smiled weakly. "What makes you think anything is..." He waved his hand over his forehead. "That's a stupid question, isn't it? Okay...okay, come here a minute, Tige."

Tige stood in front of him and allowed him to hold his hands. He seemed to need it for support.

"Well, you see, I've been doing some thinking..."

"'Bout time, ain't it?" Tige teased in an attempt to help his spirits. A dimple appeared for a second on Marvin's cheek, then disappeared.

"Yes, it is about time I started using my head for something. You know, Tige, you remember when you were sick and I had to leave you alone at times?"

"So?"

"Well I was just thinking...what would happen to you if something suddenly happened to me. I suppose that's something your mother thought a lot about too—

only we see she never came up with a solution."

"Marvin."

"Yes?"

"You sound like you plannin' on dyin'."

"What if I were, Tige? What then, for you? You'd be alone again, wouldn't you?"

"Nawl. I'd come with ya."

Marvin smiled lightly at Tige's sincerity.

"I believe you would. But that's not really the issue here. I don't have a prearranged date of departure, so let's just forget that. What I was trying to get you to see was that this isn't the perfect arrangement we have here. It's all right for me because I don't have anything to lose. But you're losing a lot by staying here. I can't send you to school, I can't buy you clothes, I can barely afford to feed you, and you can't always depend on me if you get sick again. So, I got to thinking about all that and I decided you should have something better."

"You gonna send me away, ain't cha?"

"I'm going to do what I think is best."

"I 'on't wanna go ta them people, Marvin. I 'on't care 'bout no school or clothes or nothin'."

"But *I* do. Listen, you haven't even heard me out yet. It's not an institution of any kind—it's a family. I met them and talked to them about it. They have three little girls and they'd like to have a boy. They invited us to dinner today."

"I ain't goin'."

"Don't tell me what you *ain't* gonna do!" Marvin lost his temper for a moment, then calmed down. "Tige, these are nice people. Listen, I'll make a deal with you. We won't rush this thing. So why don't we just go to dinner and you can meet them and decide whether or not you think you'll ever fit in with them. If you find you don't like them, then we'll leave and forget the whole thing. And if

you find that you *do* like them a little, then we can work
out something later on. How's that sound? It won't hurt to
try, now, would it?"

"I 'on't know. I guess not. You sho you ain't dyin'?"

"I'm positive. Hey, let's see if we can't finish this
puzzle before we leave today, okay?"

"'Kay."

Tige sat quietly with his face pressed against the
window, looking out as the cab drove past middle-class
houses, and catching glimpses of people—predominantly
black—taking advantage of the unscheduled spring
weather. Children were playing on swing sets, riding
bicycles, kicking footballs, and shooting baskets. Adults
were sitting in their yards and talking, or washing cars and
walking dogs. It was different from his own neighborhood. Everything here looked clean and wholesome,
comfortable and happy.

"It's nice out heah," Tige commented.

"Think you'd like to live here?" Marvin asked.

"You plannin' on buyin' a house?"

"You know what I mean."

"Hey, Marv, how you meet these people anyhow?
What you do, just went knockin' on they do' and asked if
they wanted a kid?"

"Something like that."

"How like that? Who is them people? How did you
find 'em and how come they want me without even seein'
me yet? . . . I *asked* you a question. . . . Marvin, where we
goin' man?"

"I already told you."

"You ain't told me everythang. You takin' me to a
orphanage, ain't cha?"

"I wouldn't do that."

"Then who is them people we goin' to then? I wanna
know."

"You'll find out in a little while. We're almost there."

"I wanna know now!"

Marvin turned his eyes out the window and continued to ignore Tige's demands. In protest, Tige threw half his body over into the front seat beside the cab driver.

"Hey, cabman, stop and let me outta heah. This man tryin' ta kidnap me."

Marvin grabbed him by his belt and yanked him back into the seat. "Will you stop that foolishness," he scolded, then chanced to catch the cab driver peering curiously at him through the rearview mirror. "He's just being silly," Marvin explained to him. "He likes a lot of attention."

"This man kidnappin' me!" Tige blurted. "Why would I wanna go someplace I 'on't know nothin' 'bout with a white man?"

"Tige, will you stop that?"

"Man, where you takin' me?"

"Right here," said the driver as he coasted to a stop in front of the walkway of a red-brick house.

"Who lives heah?" Tige asked.

"Richard Davis and his family," Marvin answered while reaching for his billfold. "Say, how much for the ride?"

"Seven-fifty."

"Here's a ten. Sorry, but I need all my change."

"Marvin?"

"Yes?"

"You say Richard Davis lives heah?"

"Yes."

"So who the heck is Richard Davis?"

"Your father."

"You lyin'!"

Marvin received his change and put in in his pocket. "You have the right to disbelieve me, but not the right to say I'm lying, especially when you don't know. I did some private-eyeing, and I found out from Miss Carrie who your father was, and I went to see him. I told him all about you, and he wants you to come live with him."

"How come you didn't tell me befo'e?"

"Because I wanted to wait till the last minute so you couldn't get away."

"I ain't goin' in dare," Tige announced crossly.

"Oh, you're going in all right. Even if I have to carry you over my shoulder. He's your father, Tige, and he wants to see you."

"Well how come after all this time? He wanted ta see me, he had 'leven years ta do it. You makin' some kinda deal with him or somethin'?"

"Yes. I made him the same deal I made you. If you two like each other, then maybe you'll want to stay with him; if not, you go back with me. It's as simple as that. I explained to him that your mother had died and that you needed help. And since it is partially his doing that you're walking the earth today, he feels that he should pitch in and work something out. But at any rate, all I'm asking for you to do is meet him, talk to him, and see what the two of you have been missing all these years. That's all. Now, you wanna go in?"

Tige glanced momentarily at the picturesque one-level house with the two-car carport and the wide, manicured front yard.

"You ain't gonna leave me 'lone with him, is you?"

"Not if you don't want me to."

"Well . . . okay," Tige finally consented.

"Hey, buddy," Marvin said to the cab driver, "tip you a buck if you come back around in—let's say—ninety minutes?"

"If I ain't on call, sure."

"Come on, Tige, let's go."

Before pressing the orange-colored light of the doorbell, Marvin turned Tige to face him. He stooped to adjust his tie and patted a patch of his hair in place.

"There, that's better. What about me? Everything okay?"

Tige looked him up and down. Marvin, with his well preserved green, pin-striped suit left over from his office days, looked every bit the big-shot lawyer or candidate for Congress.

"Piece of lint on yo' sleeve," Tige told him.

It was removed, and both faced the door. Marvin pressed the orange light and waited.

The door was opened by a woman about five-foot-five, slightly overweight but with a good figure. Her black hair hung long and curly about her shoulders, and her smile was accented by perfect white teeth and light-colored frosting on her lips. She was quite pretty as she smiled down at Tige as if he were a dear friend whom she hadn't seen in ages.

"Hello, Tige," she greeted him.

"Hey," he responded for lack of anything else to say.

She spoke just as pleasantly to Marvin and invited them in. She offered them seats and explained that her husband had to run an errand and would return later. She then introduced herself. Her name was Brenda—a nice enough name, Tige thought, that suited her well.

"Mama," came a child's voice from somewhere in another part of the house, "I cain't find my other shoe."

"Okay, I'll be right in. Excuse me, I'll be right back," she said to her company, then disappeared through a doorway.

"Well?" Marvin asked. "What do you think so far?"

"She's dynamite," Tige answered.

"That's not exactly what I was referring to," Marvin smiled.

"Hey, is all this they own house?" Tige asked as he gaped at the interior design of the living room and adjoining dining room.

"You mean whether or not they share it with another family—I wouldn't think so. Is this the first time you've ever been in a house?"

"I seen houses from the outside, but I never had a chance ta go inside befo'e."

He looked at the dining-room table decorated with a white lace tablecloth with a blue underlining and a bouquet of fresh flowers.

"You thank they did that special fo' us?"

"I wouldn't be surprised."

"Hmph. But hey, where's the *man*?"

"You heard what she said. He had something to take care of."

"On a Sunday?"

"Don't be so snoopy."

"Well, what's he like? Is he..."

"Shh, we'll talk about it later," Marvin whispered when he heard Brenda about to return.

He stood and nudged Tige to follow his example as she entered the room followed by three young ladies. They were about five inches different in height, with the tallest being an even five feet. They were all lightly tanned with their mother's characteristic long, wavy hair, and they stood in line, all pigtailed with bright ribbons and wearing pantsuits of the same design but in different colors. Brenda placed a hand on their shoulders as she introduced them.

"This," she said of the biggest one, "is Lorraine, and

this," she said of the middle-sized one, "is Amber," and the littlest one whom Tige figured to be about six or seven, was introduced as Sylvia.

"Girls, this is Mr. Stewart, and that's Tige, y'all's brother."

They all gave a shy greeting and a smile.

"Mama," Lorraine spoke up, "can he come play with us in the backyard?"

"Well, you have to ask *him* that," Brenda told her.

"Tige, you wanna come play with us? We got some swangs and a slidin' boa'd."

"I 'on't wanna mess up my suit," Tige mumbled.

"Tige, Amber's got some bluejeans that ought to fit you if you wanna change."

Tige started to decline again, but Marvin patted his arm and told him to go on. The girls escorted him away, and Brenda sat down in a cushioned chair across from Marvin.

"I thank he's afraid you're goin' to leave him."

"Well that is why we came. You and your husband must have quite an understanding with each other."

"Yes, we do. But I have to admit somethin' Mr. . . . ."

"Make it Marvin."

"Marvin, I have to admit somethin'. When Richard told me about Tige last Friday night, it really wasn't a surprise to me. I've known he existed. I didn't know his mama had died or that they were poor; I just knew that some years ago, Richard had done some playin' around and gotten himself in trouble. He tried to hide it, but some thangs you just cain't hide no matter how hard you try. And I know some women would shoot their husbands for somethin' like that, but I know my husband loves me and I believe he's learned a lesson from that one mistake. Tige is the one that got caught up in all this, and I don't thank anyone should hold anythang against him—I know I don't."

"So you're willing to take him in as one of your own?"

"I'm willin' to *try*. Richard wants to make up for the years he neglected him. I don't thank that's goin' to be too easy for him to handle alone, so that's where I come in. Tige seems nice anough. I like him already and you see the girls took to him pretty fast."

"Yes, I noticed that. Lovely little ladies you have."

"Thank you. They're angels when they're asleep. Sounds like they're havin' a good time out there. You wanna go spy?"

"Why not."

Brenda led him through to the back door where they watched and whispered unnoticed by the children.

"Look at that. I know why they're treatin' him that way. They wanna make sure he stays because they claim everybody in the world has a brother except them."

"Well, with all that going on, I don't see how he could resist," Marvin whispered while watching Tige become the center of attraction—like a lone rooster at a hen party. He sat with the girls in the double swing, was invited to try out the sliding board and a car tire that hung from a tree branch, and finally had to test ride their bicycles, each wanting him to ride hers first.

Marvin smiled at Tige's apparent dilemma. "I should have such trouble with females."

Tige rode past the door and saw Marvin watching him. He flashed a large grin, delighted with the opportunity to show Marvin how well he could ride. Marvin threw him a wave and felt a small pang of jealousy over Tige's acceptance of all these strangers.

He turned his head to find Richard standing at the kitchen window peering out.

"Good evening, Davis."

"Evening," Richard replied without looking away from the window. "I could pick him out of a crowd."

He let the curtain drop and turned to Marvin.

"Sorry I'm late. I thought I should go get him a present or something."

"He should appreciate that. Would you like me to call him in now?"

"He's—he's having fun. Don't bother just now. You and me can do a little talking in the den."

Marvin followed him into the den, where he seated himself on a brown, leather couch and refused the drink he was offered.

"Nice home you have."

"Thank you." Richard continued to stare out the window.

"He *does* look like me, doesn't he? He did when he was a baby, but more so now. He's getting along with the girls, I see."

He walked away from the window and sat opposite Marvin atop the stereo, letting one foot dangle inches above the floor.

"Is there a word for it when you're afraid of people you don't even know? Because I didn't run out to buy him a present—I already did that. I just didn't want to be here when he came. I've been drivin' around for two hours trying to get the butterflies out of my stomach and make up a speech or something and figure out some of the questions he might ask so I'll have the answers ready."

"I wish I could help you there, but I can't," said Marvin meekly. "I do have a good idea what his first question might be though. Why—after all these years?"

"That's the one, all right. Boy. Is that what he said when you told him about me?"

"'Fraid so. Richard, I hope this isn't going too fast for you. I could keep him awhile longer, but it's just that I don't have much to offer. He can't even attend school as long as he's with me. But I don't mind keeping him . . ."

"No, no," Richard waved his hand. "I want him. He's my son. Can't be putting it off any more." He sniffed softly and grinned. "It's ironic, the whole thing really. I've got three girls and I've always been wanting a boy; silly thing is I've got one, but I've never had him. Hmph. Did you and he get along pretty good?"

"After we got used to each other, it went pretty smooth."

"And you just picked him off the streets, huh?"

"Someone needed to."

"Hey, Marv!" Tige's voice rang out from beyond the den. "Where Marvin go?" he was asking someone.

Marvin looked toward Richard, who in turn took a deep breath and gave a nod.

"Marvin?"

"In here, Tige. Come on in."

"Hey, Marv, man you should've . . ." Tige appeared at the door and began talking before realizing the presence of a third person. He stopped short with his mouth open and stared.

"Tige Jackson," said Marvin, still comfortably seated, "I'd like you to meet your father, Richard Davis."

Richard stood up, started forward slightly, then stopped. He put on a shy smile and greeted his son.

"Hello, Tige."

"Tige?" Marvin's voice broke down Tige's mental barrier, enabling him to blink his eyes, close his mouth, and respond feebly.

"What?"

"Don't you know how to say hello to a person?"

"Oh. Hey," Tige said to Richard.

"Hey."

"Tige," Marvin grabbed his attention again, "he can't see your new haircut from there. Come on in."

Tige walked gradually into the room and stopped by Marvin. He gazed strongly at Richard, noticing the vaguely familiar resemblance between himself and this man.

"It's been a long time," Richard said. "I remember you still wearing diapers. Pretty big now. I...uh...I've got a basketball rack and net in the backyard. You like basketball?"

There was no response at first. Tige looked from his father to Marvin, who was trying with his eyes to encourage him to speak.

"Yeah. I like it a li'l'," Tige stated finally.

"That's good. Maybe you and me can get into a game sometime. It's murder just having a bunch of women around all the time...."

The line of conversation didn't really seem to be getting anywhere, so Richard changed it by picking up a small package from behind him and offering it to Tige.

"This is for you. Just something I thought you might like."

Tige accepted the gift-wrapped box only after receiving a go-ahead nod from Marvin.

"It's a watch," he said, holding the case open so Marvin could see.

"That's very nice. So what do you say?" urged Marvin.

Tige closed it up and thanked Richard timidly.

"You're welcome," Richard replied, then watched silently as Tige took a seat very close to Marvin and placed a hand on his leg, seemingly for security.

"You don't act like you're too thrilled to see me," Richard said.

Tige found his tongue then and used it accordingly.

"Why should I be? I ain't seen ya fo' *this* long, so what's the big deal? You got yo' pretty house and Cad'lac and everythang, and ain't never cared two cents 'bout me. And you must thank that li'l' stankin' ten-dollar watch gonna make everythang okay, but it ain't. 'Cause you prob'bly sorry Marvin dug ya up in the first place. You prob'bly wish I was dead too."

"Tige, that's enough. I think he gets the message."

Richard hung his head in shame as Tige's words lashed out against him. When Marvin smoothed the path for him, he raised it slightly and spoke.

"Okay. You can say anything about me you want to because I owe you that much. But I just want to do one thing first—I want to tell you *my* side of the story. I don't know what yo' mama might've told you—I don't know and I don't care. I can see that you hate me. I'd rather it be for a better reason than just not knowing me."

Tige sat quietly, annoyed to have to listen but willing just the same.

"Okay. It's a long story, but it's true. It's not that I never cared about you or didn't want you—I did. I just couldn't have you. Vanessa didn't want me to have you or have anything to do with you. I don't know, you might have a different picture of yo' mama than I do. I swear I never understood that girl. She and I were both kids. I used to date her some. I liked her as a *friend*, but I was never in love with her—I don't know how many times I had to tell her that. Anyway, after awhile, I met Brenda and we decided to get married. Vanessa didn't like the idea, but there wasn't anything she could do about it. Least that's what I thought at the time.

"So awhile later when Brenda was pregnant—uh, that means she was goin' to have a baby."

"I *know* what it means," Tige huffed.

"He knows quite a lot," Marvin added.

Richard shifted his sitting position so as not to face Tige directly.

"Oh. Well anyway, Brenda was about three months with Lorraine and she got this virus or something, and she had to spend some time in the hospital so they could make sure it wouldn't harm the baby any. And while she was away and I was home alone, I got this crazy idea to call up Vanessa and have her keep me company. That's where I went wrong, right then and there. I had everything I wanted in Brenda, and why I thought I needed something on the side, I don't know. But Vanessa and I got together— that was my ego getting in the way, 'cause I knew she was still crazy about me. But then we had to cut it off when Brenda came back home. And I was so ashamed of myself, I swore I'd never even see yo' mama again. So then, after three or four months ... Vanessa's callin' me up at work to tell me she's pregnant. I almost died right then. I wasn't about to give up what I had for ..."

"Me?" Tige finished the sentence incorrectly.

Richard shook his head. "I never had anything against you, honestly. I was having a rough time of it then—trying to support two families on that little paycheck of mine. I nearly went crazy trying to keep straight which baby needed what. I stuck it out for a couple of years, but I swear I was about to go out of my mind. Brenda wanted to know where all my money was going to, and Vanessa wanted me to stay around her more, saying that a boy needed more than just a part-time father. She kept hinting at me to leave my wife, but I wasn't about to do that—I love my lady. Besides, it wasn't for you she wanted me, it was herself. I found that out when I made her an offer to adopt you from her. That was the only thing I could think of that would let me give you the things you needed and keep my life together too. But Vanessa, man, she blew her top. Said if I didn't want *her*, I sure wasn't getting you. Said it wasn't going to be no half-and-half deal. So, I told her just what I felt at the time. Just because she had my baby didn't mean she owned me. I said that I'd send her money for child support every month and that I'd take you off her hands if she thought she couldn't handle things.

"Like I said before, it must not've been you she had in mind then, because she slapped my face, called me every name she could think of and told me not to ever come back. And I have to admit I was so glad to get that extra pressure off my back, I really didn't care one way or the other. But I did send her money—twenty dollars a week—until one day one of the checks came back. Vanessa had moved without leaving a forwarding address. I figured she had met someone else or probably was just doing so well that she didn't need my help any more. I thought about coming to find you once, just to see how you were growing up. I guess I don't have too much of an excuse for not doing *that* much. But I remember how Vanessa *was* that last day, so I just didn't bother."

He paused a moment to take off his glasses and wipe away a bothersome eyelash. Without his glasses, his eyes looked tired and rather sad. They were dark, slightly wide and spacious. They were Tige's eyes.

He slipped his glasses back on and looked at Tige.

"I'm sorry about yo' mama dying—I really am. I don't

know if I could take her place with you or not, but I *am* yo' daddy and I'm not ashamed to let anybody know it now. I hope that answers most of yo' questions for you. I swear it's all the truth."

He had completed his story and looked up at Tige and Marvin. The tale seemed to have softened Tige somewhat; the expression on his face was less hostile. If the story hadn't been an honest and truthful one, then it had to be the best-told fairytale he'd ever heard. Tige glanced at Marvin, who also seemed to be at a loss for words.

"Scuse me, y'all," Lorraine stuck her head through the door, breaking the silence. "Daddy, mama said dinner ready, if anybody int'rested."

Richard sat lamely on top of the stereo watching Tige.

"Are you hungry?" he asked him.

Tige neglected to answer.

"I don't know about him, but I'm starved." Marvin stood up and Tige stood with him. "Mind if we wash up a little first?"

"Course not. I'll show you the bathroom."

Tige waited until they were left alone. Then he closed the door securely so he and Marvin could talk.

"You believe all that?" he asked.

"It's not whether or not *I* believe it," Marvin replied as he took advantage of a pink bar of soap and warm water. "It's whether *you* believe it."

"But he try ta make like it was all my mama's fault."

"Tige, what's past is past. Both your mother and father were young then. They both made mistakes. You and your mother suffered for it. There's nothing we can do about your mother, but *you*, you're quite a different story."

"So you want me ta come live heah?"

"I want you to wash your hands so we can go eat."

Tige moved to the sink and dunked his hands under the water.

"I 'on't thank I wanna live heah. I 'on't like him no way."

"On what grounds do you base your contempt?"

"What?"

"I said, you can't judge a person in fifteen minutes. Remember, you weren't too crazy about me at first. Come on, that's enough. You don't want to wash the color off."

Tige and Marvin walked into the dining room, which was busy with chatter and movement.

"Heah they come, Mama."

"Oh, good. Marvin, you can sit here, and, Tige, right next to you."

They took one side of the table, the girls were squeezed comfortably together on the other side, and their hosts were at both ends.

"I hope you'll like my cookin'," Brenda said while passing around plates and heaping out portions of potato salad, ham, and all the trimmings. "Anythang you see you don't like, just let me know."

"Everything looks just fine to me," Marvin smiled.

Everyone dug into their meals except for father and son. Richard tapped a hunk of potato with his fork, glancing from time to time at Tige. Tige was nowhere near his plate. He sat back in his chair, looking everywhere but in his father's direction.

"Eat up, Tige," Marvin told him. "It's good."

"I ain't hungry."

"You *should* be."

"But I ain't."

"Suit yourself. He's just getting over being sick,"

Marvin informed Brenda. "He usually can eat like a horse."

"Oh, one of those," Brenda grinned. "That sounds like Sylvia. I don't know where that girl can put so much. Look at that plate already. She can put it away, cain't she? I believe she's got a hole in her stomach."

"Bottomless pit," Lorraine teased. But her little sister ate her food and ignored all the comments.

"Tige, you sure you don't want anythang to eat? I've got some Jell-O with fruit cocktail and some cake for dessert."

"You can wrap it all up in some 'luminum foil and I can take it home with me."

"Home?" Richard blurted. He looked past Tige to glare at Marvin, then dropped his fork and excused himself from the table.

"What's a madder with him?" asked Tige.

"If you really wanted to know," said Marvin, "you'd ask him."

There was silence after that until the girls whispered a short conversation and came to the conclusion that they had finished supper and would like their dessert in the backyard.

"Why don't you run along with them," Marvin suggested. "Go on."

Tige went with them reluctantly as they stopped off in the kitchen to load up and continued on outside.

"I really enjoyed the meal, Mrs...."

"Brenda," she corrected him. "I just wish that Tige had eaten somethin'. He's thin anough already."

"You need any help with the dishes?" Marvin asked.

"No, no thank you. The luxuries of havin' a dishwasher."

"Well, you suppose your husband's in the den?"

"Yeah, I thank that's where I saw him head. I hope you can pep him up or somethin'. I hate to see him carryin' around that long face."

Marvin rose from the table and left the dining room. He walked into the den where Richard was stretched out on a reclining chair, his glasses in one hand and his forehead in the other.

"Headache?" Marvin startled him.

"What? Oh, no. I...I was just thinkin'—*tryin'* to think."

He slipped his glasses back on and returned his chair to a sitting position.

"Maybe it's just my imagination, but I don't think he likes me any."

"Well he wasn't all that fond of me at first either. But we finally got it together. It took a little time, certainly more than a few minutes."

"Yeah, yeah, I know, I know. But what was that about him taking his dinner home with him? Didn't you tell him he was coming here to live?"

Marvin shrugged his shoulders and went to examine a mother and child painted on black velvet.

"Forgive me—I'm a coward. I didn't have the heart to tell him. It's good I didn't—otherwise I'd never have gotten him through the door. At least he's here now and he's seen and met you and your family. It should give him something to think about when I tell him this is it. I got him here—your job is to *keep* him here."

"The thing is," Richard said after a short silence, "will he let go as easy as you're doing?"

Marvin looked away and back toward the painting.

"Easy, huh? I wish it were. But if I do my part right, and you do yours right, then there shouldn't be anything to worry about. I hope."

"'Scuse me," Brenda appeared at the door. "Marvin, did you call for a cab? There's one out here blowin'."

"Ah, I guess I did. I hate to eat and run, but uh, under the circumstances, I think it's as good a time as any to say goodbye to him."

Marvin stepped into the living room and saw Tige whizzing past on his way to one of the bedrooms.

"Cab heah, Marvin," he said. "I gotta go change."

"Tige, wait." Marvin tried to stop him but he was moving too fast. "I'll . . . I'll catch him outside."

Tige rushed quickly to shed the borrowed jeans and to get into his own pants. He had them zipped at the same moment he heard the front door click shut. Snatching up his jacket, he ran out, taking the shorter route through the back door. When he came around the side of the house, he stopped only for a second to watch Marvin shake hands with Richard.

"Hey, Marv, wait up!"

Marvin stood alongside the cab, apparently anxious to leave.

"Thought I was going to leave without saying goodbye?" he smiled.

Tige confronted him with confusion. "What? What you talkin' 'bout?"

"I'm talking about this is it. I told you I'd do what I thought was best, didn't I?"

"But you said . . . you said we was just comin' heah fo' dinner, and all I had ta do was meet 'em. You didn't say I had ta stay heah. You said we was gonna go right back home . . ."

"Tige," Marvin stopped him from going any further, "you *are* home. This is where you belong, and this is where I want you to stay."

"But I 'on't like it heah. I 'on't like them."

"Don't do that, Tige. Don't lie. I know what's going on up in that mind of yours, but it just can't be anymore. You don't belong with me. It was nice while it lasted, and I was happy for the company. But there's so much more for you here. You get a nice house in a good neighborhood, clothes, toys, a chance to go to school and grow up healthy—and look behind you.... Go ahead, look."

Tige slowly let his eyes wander momentarily away from Marvin to glance back over his shoulder. He saw his father leaning against a tree a short distance away. And beyond him was Brenda, standing on the porch, shadowed by her daughters. Tige felt them all calling to him in his mind, beckoning him to stay.

"You see?" Marvin drew his attention. "A ready-made family, all in one day. What more could you possibly want?"

Tige gazed up into his eyes with tears starting to form.

"Do me a favor, Tige, and promise me you'll stay here."

Tige shook his head defiantly.

"Tige, I didn't bring you all the way out here just to drag you back with me. Now I was trying to do this the easy way so I wouldn't hurt your feelings, but if you really must know, I was getting tired of the whole setup. I admit I didn't mind it at first, but after awhile a person *can* get tired of some things, *and* some people. I just can't have you holding onto my coattail anymore. So that's why I went through all this. I thought you might at least be grateful that I didn't just kick you out with no place to go."

"You lyin'," Tige accused angrily.

Marvin looked down at him with the menacing stare that had always been effective in showing he meant business.

"And *what* if I'm not? If you don't want to stay here, then that's fine with me. You do what you want. But just don't come running back to me, because I don't want you. You can understand that well enough, can't you? I've done what I can for you. If you're stupid enough to louse it up, go right ahead, but if you know what's good for you, you'll stay put."

Marvin turned and started to enter the cab.

"Marvin," Tige called to him softly.

Marvin stopped for a second, then climbed into the cab without looking back. Tige watched as the cab pulled away from the curb and stared after it until it had disappeared around the corner. Then, dropping his head, Tige turned slowly and walked back toward the house.

Spring had captured winter's imagination, and summer was fast approaching. Dogwoods had blossomed and turned the trees into white, flimsy-headed creatures.

But for Marvin, the days had only made themselves into weeks and the weeks had stretched painfully into months. He had sulked miserably for two weeks after Tige's departure. He had tried hard to forget him, and he would succeed for a while until some scrawny, bushy-headed little boy who looked like Tige from a distance brought back memories.

There had been no communication with him at all, not one word of how he was doing. Marvin rarely found anything to smile about, and he loathed the rainy days that often found him spinning an empty liquor bottle and staring up at the picture puzzle that hung on the wall. He even found himself dreading to return home at all because he knew that there was nothing there for him.

It just wasn't fair to be so all alone. He hadn't minded it before Tige came, but now it was much too obvious. He felt he needed a companion of some kind, but he wasn't that fond of dogs and cats. He finally ended up with two inexpensive friends that were gold-bodied and excellent swimmers. He borrowed his and Tige's names and turned them backward, so that the small fish was named Egit and the larger one, Nivram. Not big on conversation, either of them, but they managed to give Marvin the imagined sense of friendship that he needed.

His friends were nice to look at and never gave him any back talk. They didn't even complain to him about changing their water—though they probably would have if they could have.

It was a day in the middle of June—a warm Friday afternoon. When Marvin returned home from grocery shopping, three little girls were playing a game of hopscotch a few feet from his home. They smiled shyly at him and said, "Hey." He tried to picture where he'd seen them before. But then, a lot of black kids looked the same to him, so he shrugged it off and headed up the stairs.

When he reached for the doorknob with the key in his hand, he noticed that the door wasn't fully closed. He hoped he wasn't going completely daft; he was sure he had locked it when he left. Then he heard a sound from within his apartment that frightened him into thinking that perhaps someone was waiting inside to jump him. Not wanting to take on an attacker who might be armed, he decided to tiptoe back down the stairs and give whoever it was a chance to escape with whatever he was after.

Marvin turned to leave and saw the girls up the street still playing. He studied their yellowy-brown skin and the long flapping pigtails on each and his memory soon fit the pieces together. Their last name was Davis. And that could only mean that one certain person had returned to clump about in his apartment. It just had to be. . . .

He burst through the door, dropping his packages on the floor. Tige spun around as the noise startled him, and his face registered about as much surprise as Marvin's.

They stared at each other a few seconds, then Tige moved from in front of the fishbowl on the kitchen cabinet.

"Yo' fishes' wadder need changin', Marv," he said.

"Ye-ah, yeah—I—I know," Marvin stammered.

Tige turned to watch the fish again.

"I thank I might like ta git me some fish. Hey, I bet the big one's you and the li'l' one's me, right?" He turned to see if Marvin was agreeing with him, but Marvin was still dumbfounded as he stood limply at the door.

"What's the madder with you? You seen this spook befo'e," Tige smiled, then added his greeting. "Hey, Marvin."

The initial shock wore off, and Marvin returned to normal. "Hi, Tige," he smiled back.

"Dare ya go.... Did I scare ya? No, *you* sked *me*. I didn't know *what* that was come crashin' through the do' like that."

"Oh...I—uh—thought it was burglars."

"Oh. You made a mess though, didn't cha?"

Tige went before Marvin and began picking his groceries up for him.

"You broke yo' eggs, Marv."

"That's okay. I like 'em scrambled."

"On the flo'?"

Tige gathered up everything and set it on the table.

"How long have you been here?" Marvin asked as he closed the door.

"I 'on't know. Not too long. I 'on't thank. I wa'n't sure you'd come home befo'e we left, but I decided ta wait fo' awhile and see."

"When I first started up here," said Marvin, "I saw the girls and I *thought* they looked familiar. Just couldn't place them though. Were you all headed someplace?"

"Just heah. See, they don't hardly git a chance ta ride the bus and they don't even know they way downtown. So whenever I go somewhere where I 'on't mind havin' 'em around, I just brang 'em with me. Uh, can I have a doughnut—I'll put yo' groc'ry up fo' ya."

"Go ahead," Marvin consented. He leaned against the door with his arms folded to watch Tige as he went in a triangle from the table, to the refrigerator, to the cabinet, and back to the table.

"I started ta come see ya sooner, but I been busy, you know—git'in' used ta everybody and git'in' started in school and everythang. I started ta write you too, but then, I'on't write all that good yet. I thought you might've wanted ta write me though, or call on the phone. The number's in the book. But I guess you just didn't wanna bug me or you prob'bly thought I was mad at cha fo' just about cussin' me out that day. I know you didn't mean it—did cha?"

"No. No, I didn't."

"Didn't thank so. Can I have some milk too?"

"Course. How 'bout pouring me a glass while you're at it?"

"Okay. . . . Marvin, don't you *ever* wash dishes?"

"Well, I just got a little behind in my housework."

Marvin sat down at the table with his elbows up and his hands clasped beneath his chin. He gazed at the neat, clean, well-dressed young man who seemed to have grown about an inch taller. The slim little figure was dressed in a blue and white striped tank top covered by a red shirt-jacket, pressed flared blue jeans, white sneakers, and a belt with a buckle in the form of two hands shaking soulfully. He looked quite dapper, except for the white powder around his mouth from the doughnuts. He brought Marvin his milk and sat down to finish the doughnut he had started.

"I see your appetite hasn't been damaged any. You look like you've gained a little weight."

"I did. Fo' pounds. And guess what."

"What?"

"I told ya ta guess, but I'll tell ya anyway. I grew three-quarders inches tall."

"Taller—and I noticed. They've really been taking care of you, haven't they?"

"Yeah. 'Cause I git ta eat three whole times a day."

"Well, I know about when you were with me, but didn't you ever have three square meals a day?"

"Nope. I sometimes ate breakfast and maybe a biscuit or a piece of candy or somethin' fo' lunch. But I never had a whole plate of food fo' everytime."

"Eating the right foods is good for you. I think now I should've been a little more helpful with that. You look pretty healthy now."

"I oughtta be. I been to the docta 'bout twen'y-million times. Everytime I turned around, seemed like I was goin' to the docta fo' somethin' or other. First time was ta git a checkup and the docta said I had maltrition."

"Malnutrition?"

"What? Oh—yeah, you prob'bly right. He told me what it was but I fa'got. Then he made up a list of foods I had ta eat and I have ta take a vitamin everyday too.

"Then I had ta go git some shots—vaccinations—and I went to the dentist—I had some cavities but he fixed 'em. And guess what else."

"What?"

Tige beamed proudly as if it were truly a great

accomplishment as he announced the removal of his tonsils.

"Really? How long were you in the hospital this time?"

"Just a coupla days."

"Were you afraid?"

"Nawl, not really, because Lorraine had her tonsils out befo'e and she told me what it was like. At first, I wa'n't suppose ta talk, then when I could, I sounded funny. But now I sound just like me ag'in, don't I?"

Marvin smiled and nodded, keeping what he felt to be the truth to himself. Tige didn't really sound like himself. The voice itself was the same, but the character of it had changed dramatically. Now it was pleasant and cheerful, and the words came forth gaily, without frowning, and with the noticeable lack of need to curse.

He had changed in other ways also. His skin was a tone lighter—perhaps just from more regular washing, and the sad circles below his eyes had faded, leaving him with a face lit brighter than it had ever been before.

"How are you doing in school?" Marvin questioned.

"Not too bad. I'm 'pose ta be in the sixth grade, but I 'on't know anough fo' that yet. When I first went ta school, they wanted ta give me a test ta see how much I knew and figure out what grade I was 'pose ta be in. But then I had ta tell 'em I couldn't read or write—'cept fo' that li'l' bit you taught me—so they said that I'd have ta start off in the first grade. But daddy said 'no-o-o way', 'cause he knew kids would make fun of me and I'd prob'bly end up git'in' in a lotta fights or somethin'. Anyway, they got this friend of Brenda's who teach fifth grade at school ta tutor me. She spends a hour and a half with me alone everyday after school, and durin' the rest of the day, I git ta sit in on her class. I'm her aide. I git ta pass out books and take up papers and all that, and while I'm sit'in' in her class, I be list'nin' to what be goin' on when they have discussions. So that means that I'm learnin' stuff I should've already learned, and some I should be learnin' anyway. It's kinda hard sometimes tryin' ta understand some of that stuff, but Miss Daniels said I shouldn't worry about tryin' ta learn everythang all at once. She said I'm doin' pretty good right now not ta have hardly been ta school that much. She said I'm ready fo' the second grade already and if I work on through the summer—she'll be able ta spend whole days with me—she said I might make it ta the third-grade level by September."

"Oh, that's pretty good. I'm very proud of you. Didn't really think you'd care that much for books and bells."

"It ain't so bad. It's fun sometimes. We git ta do a lot of stuff and go on field trips. That's real cool."

"Glad to hear you're doing so well. How about your sisters? You get along with them all right?"

"Yeah, they okay. Man, them gulls crazy. They wait on me hand and foot, fix me food, and loan me thangs, clean up my room fo' me, and they take up fo' me if anybody try ta tease me 'bout not bein' smart. They okay, but it's one thang I 'on't like they try ta git me ta do—they keep tryin' ta git me to call Brenda 'Mama.' I tried it a coupla times. I said it real low so she couldn't heah me, but it just don't sound right comin' out. I can call my daddy 'Daddy,' because that's who he is, but Brenda—she 'on't mind no way."

"Yeah, well she struck me as a very understanding person....Hey, that's a neat-looking belt buckle you're wearing."

Tige grabbed his buckle and lifted it up away from his stomach.

"My uncle gave it to me. You know somethin'? I got relatives I never knew I had. I got two grandmamas—one

is a step-grandmama—and two granddaddies—one of
them is a step too. Then I got three uncles, fo' ainnies, and
about a thousand cousins and nephews and nieces. Man, I
swear.... Oh yeah, that reminds me..."

Tige reached somewhere inside his jacket and pulled
out a three-by-five, golden-trimmed picture frame,
showing that at least one thing hadn't changed—he still
managed to keep secret compartments in his clothes.

"They had pictures made of me," he said, as he
presented Marvin with a colorful portrait of himself.
"Daddy had a whole bunch of 'em made and gave just
about all of 'em away, but I saved that one fo' you."

Marvin smiled and eyed it carefully. "You know who
this looks like?" he asked.

"Who?"

Marvin looked from the picture back to Tige.

"Oh-h-h! You mean *me*," Tige laughed. "Yeah, well I
thank it looks a li'l' like me, yeah."

"I appreciate your thinking of me. Thank you."

"You welcome. But you gotta git some made of you
so I can have one."

"Well, I'll see what I can do about it."

Marvin looked back at the picture. "That's a real
sharp jacket there. I suppose you wouldn't need any of the
stuff you left here, would you? I never bothered to throw
them out."

"Man, don't talk ta me 'bout no clothes. I got so much
stuff, I 'on't even know what ta do. They bought me
everythang. I got coats and jackets, and pants and shirts,
shoes, socks, underwear—you name it. Plus, I can wear
some of Amber's clothes too. I *would* like my skates back
though, if you got 'em."

"I'm sorry. Things got a little tight. I had to pawn
them."

"Oh. That's okay, I can buy my own. I git two dollars

a week fo' 'lowance, and I git extra when I mow the lawn
and trim the hedges. I'm savin' up so I can buy me a
camera. My uncle got a real pretty one that takes a lot of
dif'rent kinda pictures. He said when I git mine, he gonna teach me how ta use it. You know, him and my daddy
look just alike."

"Are they twins?"

"I thank so. 'Cept fo' he's older and a li'l' taller and
lighter."

"You haven't told me yet—how are you and your
father getting along?"

"All right, I guess."

"Sounds like there's a little bit more to it than that.
Having problems?"

"Nawl, not really. It's just that . . . I like him and all—
we have some good times tagether sometimes. Like he
takes me ta ballgames and we play basketball in the
backyard against the gulls—girls . . . but . . ."

"But what?"

"Well, it's just that I 'on't git ta see him that much. I
have ta go ta school and he have ta go ta work. Sometimes
I don't even git ta see him in the mo'nin'. And when he
comes home, all he wanna do is eat and look at television. I
'on't git ta sleep with him and talk to him at night like I did
with you. And even on the weekends, it ain't that much
bedder 'cause he got friends he like ta go visit or they
come ta him, plus he got fo' other people at home ta be
with besides me. I guess I'm just used ta bein' with just one
person and not a whole family. I like it one ta one. . . . Marvin?"

"Yes?"

"I know I used ta bug you a lot, but would you mind if
I came ta spend some time with ya? Like on weekends or
after school?"

Marvin masked his enthusiasm successfully and answered him. "I don't mind at all. It does get a bit quiet around here at times. I don't mind at all. But there's no telling what times I'll be home, you know. We could pick certain days, though, I guess."

"Yeah. It'd be good if you had a telephone—then I could call you everyday."

"That's an idea. I do have an old phone—maybe it wouldn't cost that much to have it reconnected."

"I can help you pay fo' it with my 'lowance."

"We'll leave your allowance out of it. I should be able to swing it myself. May take awhile though."

"That'd be good if you could do that. Then when you feel like it, you could call me, or when I need somebody ta talk to, I could call you. You 'on't want yo' milk, I'll drank it."

Marvin pushed his glass into Tige's hand. Tige drank half of it and burped softly.

"'Scuse me. I'm gonna have ta stop drankin' so much milk. It gives me gas. You oughtta see what *choc'lit* milk makes me do—whew."

Tige paused a moment to survey his milk and to make sure that the speck of something he saw was on the outside of the glass and not inside. He finished his inspection with favorable results and glanced casually up at Marvin, catching him eye-to-eye—something he hadn't done since he'd arrived. He stared first, then regained his voice.

"Why you always do that?"

"Do what?"

"Smile like that. You do it all the time, ever since I known ya. You always smile like that."

Marvin put his hand to his cheek, covering the left side of his mouth.

"I guess I never noticed. I don't carry a mirror around

with me all the time. I suppose it's just an involuntary action.... Then again, it may simply mean I'm pleased."

Tige nodded his acceptance of the answer. "You ever missed me any?"

"I missed you a great deal."

"I guess I missed you too. A whole lot at first, but everybody kept tellin' me not ta keep thankin' about it, and that I'd git over it."

"And did you—get over it?"

Tige shrugged his shoulders. "I 'on't know. After I was dare fo' awhile, I got used to it.... Marvin, you still like me?"

"Why do you ask?"

"I 'on't know. I guess 'cause everythang just seems so dif'rent. When I first walked through that do' I could tell it. I done got so used ta chandelier lights and carpets on the flo' and paintin's on the walls.... This place, it just don't seem the same no mo'e."

"What about me?" asked Marvin.

"You—you seem dif'rent too. You the same, I know, but you still seem dif'rent. I 'on't understand it."

"I think I might know. It's just like two ugly ducklings living in a pond. But in actuality, only one is really a duck, the other is a swan. And you see what happens is that the ugly duckling that's a swan, one day he leaves the pond. And while he's away, he grows, gets his new feathers, meets other swans, and learns what it's like to be a swan. Okay, so one day he thinks to himself he should go back to the pond and see how his old pal is doing. And when he gets there, he finds that even though he's become a big beautiful bird with all his gracefulness and good looks, his old pal is still just an ugly old duck, living in the same muddy pond with his same old ways. Now we both know that a duck and a swan aren't quite the same thing and they kind of look dumb together, but that doesn't mean that it can't happen. Maybe they won't ever be quite the same as when they were both ugly ducklings, but you can't deny that they once had something pretty strong going on. And it shouldn't matter *what* kind of changes they've gone through, a little bit of that something should still be with both of them. It *is* with me. What about you?"

Tige nodded with a shy smile. "That's cute. I was wond'rin' if you could still do that—explain thangs like that. Yeah, it's still with me."

Tige picked up his milk and finished it off.

"You hung up the puzzle," he noted.

"Yeah. I've been wanting to for some time. I've got another one I'm working on now. Well, not just yet. I haven't even taken it out of the sack."

"Marvin, you like doin' thangs like that by yo'self?"

"You mean putting together puzzles?"

"Not just the puzzles—I mean everythang. I used ta wonder about that a lot. I sometimes wondered if I wa'n't heah ta talk to you or help you with yo' puzzle or eat with you, I wondered how you could stand ta do all that all by yo'self. I figured you been doin' it all the long befo'e you met me, but I still wonder—don't you ever git lonely?"

"Well, I've—I've grown pretty accustomed to my privacy," Marvin answered, feeling that that was sufficient.

"Well, I know 'bout privacy. I like it too sometimes. But not *all* the time. People got ta git lonely sometimes. I know I did when I didn't never have nobody ta play with or talk to. Marv, don't you *ever* git lonely?"

"Well . . . yes, yes, I suppose I do sometimes."

"Then why you do it?"

"Do what—be lonely?"

"Nawl. Why you lock yo'self up in this 'partment?

You livin' on a whole block with no neighbors. Don't you like people?"

"What? That's quite a question to be asking—don't I like people. Of course I like people."

"Well, the way you act, you either don't like 'em or you sked of 'em."

Marvin shifted his eyes quickly to the goldfish bowl. Tige watched his face for a moment then pursued the topic.

"That's it, ain't it, Marv? That's why you never got along with yo' chilluns, ain't it? And that's why you quit yo' job because of them folks at yo' office. Is that why you ain't got no friends? You sked they gonna treat you bad? If they was fo' real friends, they wouldn't do that. . . . Marv?"

Marvin sighed and left the table to go feed his fish. "Is that what you want to major in?" he asked with his back to Tige. "Psychology? You should, you know. You're very good at it. . . ." Marvin sat the box of fishfood down and turned back to Tige. "Only two people in my life I can really say never treated me like dirt, and that was Cathy . . . and you."

"I used ta be pretty rotten ta ya at first, though."

"No, not me. I believe you just had it in for the whole world. I was pleased with myself when I asked you to stay. I mean—knowing that I let something happen, not because anyone was forcing me or telling me I ought to do it. I did it on my own because I wanted to. And I'm pretty sure if I had it to do over. . . ." He nodded and smiled.

"But, Marvin, it ain't right ta just turn off *all* people. Don't you want *no* friends?"

"Tige, you're getting at something. What is it?"

"Nothin'. I was just wond'rin' wouldn't you want ta meet some people. Like, it's a teacher at school—she ain't hardly got nobody either. She looks kinda yo' type. I 'on't mean fo' ya ta git married. I know how you feel 'bout that. But I thank she might make you a good friend. And another thang—if you wanna, I know where you could git a job. Daddy said they got a coupla openin's where he work. You could meet a lot of people that way and git you a new 'partment and . . ."

"And rejoin civilization. Is that what you're saying?" Marvin said with a smirk on his face. "You *are* a swan. You want the duck to dive into your pond with you. I've thought about it a thousand times. You can see what my answer always turned out to be. Maybe someday, who knows, I might just pick up and leave this hole. Maybe someday I'll change into a swan too. But until I do, you'll just have to accept me the way I am."

Tige looked away from him and fingered his empty glass. "I didn't mean nothin' by it. I just wanted ya ta be happy," he murmured.

Marvin grabbed a chair and sat down beside him. He put out his hand and raised Tige's chin up with his finger.

"Hey, right now, the only thing in the world that could make me happy is to see you smile."

He watched Tige's watery eyes, then the corners of his mouth as they painfully turned upwards. Tige stood and wrapped his arms around Marvin's neck.

"You scare me when you do thangs like that. But we still friends, ain't we?"

"Of course we are. I just get carried away at times. Don't let anything I say scare you."

"Well it ain't what you say, it's how you say it. But you right. If I tried ta change ya, you wouldn't be you no mo'e. Who would you be?"

"I'd be a tired old man in a two-hundred-dollar suit with a job that I hate and friends I can't stand. We don't wanna do that to me, do we?"

"Nawl, guess not." Tige pulled away and took a position on Marvin's lap with an arm still around his neck. "You need a shave, Marv. You git'in' fuzzy."

"I'll get around to it sooner or later."

"Have it done by Sunday?"

"Why Sunday?"

"Special day. My birthday."

"Your—well I'll be. Twelve, right?"

"Yeah. I used ta didn't thank I'd ever make it this far. But I did. And you and me, we gonna pack a picnic and spend all day long at—guess."

"Six Flags."

"Ri-i-ight."

"And the Scream Machine?"

"But of course. You brang yo' good stomach. Daddy said he'd pick you up heah and drive us over dare, or if you wanna, I can meet you downtown and we can ride the bus."

"Well, I suppose the sooner we get there, the more time we'll have for everything, so maybe we should let your father chauffeur us around."

"Okay. And after that, you come home with me fo' dinner and git some birthday cake. And I wanna show you my room too. I got posters up that I drew myself. Did you know I could draw?"

"No, I didn't."

"I didn't either at first. I knew I could color, but I never had a whole lotta pencils and paper that I could play with befo'e. Man, I got a whole bunch of stuff now."

Tige pulled his arm from around Marvin's neck and turned his own oversized watch face up on the back of his wrist.

"What time is that?"

"Can't you tell time yet?"

"Yeah, I can tell time, but when it gits between the numbers like that, it mix me up."

Marvin held Tige's wrist and pointed out the time with his thumb.

"It's five, ten, fifteen, sixteen, seventeen minutes past four. Do you have to leave now?"

"Yeah, we gotta go catch the bus. 'Pose ta git dare 'bout fo'-thirty. You wanna walk us to the bus stop?"

"I'm afraid I have to visit the bathroom first."

"Short or long visit?"

"Long."

"In that case...." Tige got up and headed for the door. With his hand on the knob, he stopped and turned.

"Goodbye, goldfish, I'll see y'all later." Then he looked into Marvin's twinkling blue eyes. "Marv?"

"Yes?"

"Will you laugh if I tell ya somethin'?"

"That depends whether I think it's funny."

"Oh, well it's just somethin' that I thought I oughtta tell ya in case you didn't know." He paused, trying to be brave about it. "Marvin...I love ya," he said very bashfully, then shrugged his shoulders. "Least you didn't laugh."

"Was I supposed to?"

"Nawl. But where I come from, if a guy said he loved somebody, everybody thought it was sissy. But my daddy said that if you love somebody, even if it's another guy, it don't madder what other people thank. Ain't none of they business noway. And like, I never got the chance ta tell my mama to her face, but you know, mamas know that kind of stuff anyway. But just in case you wa'n't sure—I thought I'd tell ya."

"Tige, I can't even remember the last time I've heard those words. Thank you for letting me know. And I love you too."

Tige blushed, then opened the door.

"I gotta go. Be ready 'bout ten a'clock, Sunday. And don't worry 'bout a present—that's what Brenda told me ta tell ya. But really, goldfish don't cost that much, do they? Bye-bye, see ya, Marv."

"See ya Sunday."

Marvin sat for a moment and watched the closed door, then he went to the window to look out. Tige was breaking up his sisters' hopscotch game. He turned to the window and pointed as he said something to the girls. The girls all smiled and waved up at Marvin, who waved back. Then the four grabbed each others' hands and trotted away down the street to catch their bus.

Marvin let the curtain drop and walked past the table to pick up Tige's picture. The warm, sunny face smiled up at him, making him feel suddenly more alive. Already he was thinking about what he should wear on Sunday, and in what box he had packed his telephone. After remembering he had to use the bathroom, he returned to the living room to find a suitable place for Tige's picture. It ended up on the table in front of the radio. Marvin sat to admire it again, smiling happily as he did. It felt beautiful to have him back again.